"I...uh...hired a typist."

His agent snorted over the phone. "You're lying."

"No, really I did." He and Leigh hadn't exactly talked about payment, except for his brief mention of it at the haunted hike, but he certainly planned on compensating her for her time and help. Of course, he'd rather show her his gratitude in other ways, like taking her out on a real date, telling her how wonderful she was and helping to erase some of the pain in her past.

"From what agency?" Clive still sounded suspicious.

"No agency. She's just a woman who lives here in Brookhollow, next door to the B and B." It was such an understatement, Logan was almost embarrassed by the lie. But what could he tell Clive? That he was getting help from a woman he was falling in love with in the small town? Clive would for sure give up on him, thinking he'd lost his mind.

"Not the same woman who pushed you off a ladder?"

"Actually, yes."

Clive laughed. "Wow, way to call in the guilt favor."

Dear Reader,

Love can often be found when we're not looking for it. After painful past experiences, it is sometimes tempting to go through life unaware of the wonderful opportunities around us. But some opportunities, like love, refuse to be ignored. Love doesn't care that you have life plans, goals that you may be working toward or dreams that you might be chasing. It doesn't care that your heart may still be mending from a previous tear. And it doesn't care if the timing just isn't right. In this story about Logan and Leigh, love is oblivious to the fact that these two shouldn't fall in love, and it happens anyway.

In this story, both Leigh and Logan are searching for a family of their own, without stopping to realize that together they could have a family and the love they'd never thought possible and had already given up on. I hope you enjoy this story about persevering in the face of heartache and taking that one last chance that just might be the right one.

Hugs,

Jennifer

HEARTWARMING

Falling for Leigh

Jennifer Snow

HARLEQUIN® HEARTWARMING™

Recycling programs for this product may not exist in your area.

ISBN-13: 978-0-373-36692-7

Falling For Leigh

This edition published by arrangement with Harlequin Books S.A.

For questions and comments about the quality of this book, please contact us at CustomerService@Harlequin.com.

Printed in U.S.A.

JENNIFER SNOW

lives in Edmonton, Alberta, with her husband and four-year-old son. She is a member of the Writers Guild of Alberta, the Romance Writers of America, the Canadian Author Association and shewrites.org. She is also a regular blogger on the Harlequin Heartwarming Authors site and is a contributing writer for *Mslexia* magazine and *RWR*. She has offered online courses on writing sweet romance through several RWA local chapters and has written articles for *Avenue* magazine. An active volunteer with Frontier College, she is an advocate for literacy programs worldwide. More information can be found on her website, www.jennifersnowauthor.com.

Books by Jennifer Snow

HARLEQUIN HEARTWARMING

21—THE TROUBLE WITH MISTLETOE
32—WHAT A GIRL WANTS

Acknowledgments

This book would not have happened so soon
if not for the support of my amazing husband.
Reagan, I can't thank you enough for giving me the
opportunity to do what I love and for believing in
me more than anyone. Thanks a million times to
my agent, Stephany Evans, whose happy faces on
my manuscripts are what give me the strength to
face the tough critiques, as well. And as always, this
book wouldn't shine as brightly without the input
from my amazing editor, Victoria Curran.
So thank you all again for the love and support.

And finally, a big thank-you to Adoption Options for
the resources and examples of Birth Mom letters
that both broke and restored my heart.

Dedication

For Cheryl—"Courage doesn't always roar.
Sometimes courage is the quiet voice at the end
of the day saying 'I will try again tomorrow.'"
—MaryAnne Radmacher

CHAPTER ONE

"WHAT IS THAT NOISE?" Logan Walters asked through clenched teeth. He paced the hardwood floor in his room at the Brookhollow Inn, the room phone cradled to his ear. His laptop sat open on the antique writing desk, and papers were strewn about the bed. Discarded, rolled balls of yellow legal-pad paper lay near the trash can in the corner of the room. So much for the peace and quiet he'd been expecting from the small town in the middle of New Jersey. He'd been making just as much progress in his sublet studio apartment in Manhattan as he was here in Brookhollow.

None.

"I'm not sure what you mean, Mr. Walters," the Brookhollow Inn's new owner, Rachel Harper, said. "My children aren't running through the hallways of the guest quarters again, are they?"

"No, not today." That had been yesterday's distraction. He couldn't believe the bed-and-breakfast was home to so many kids. Funny, they'd forgotten to mention it on their newly designed website. He suspected complaints about noise were common now.

He ran a hand through his hair, which reached the back of his shirt collar. Past due for a cut.

Man, he missed the nice, quiet, little old lady that used to own the place. Had he known of the switch in ownership the year before, he certainly wouldn't have come.

"I don't hear anything here at the desk. What kind of noise is it?" she asked.

"It's a hammering sound." How could she not hear the deafening vibrations echoing off the walls?

"Our renovations have been complete for quite some time."

He picked up on the note of pride in her voice.

Yes, their renovations—he'd noticed them, too. New paint, new windows, new tiled roof...improvements for sure, but he'd been relieved to see they hadn't messed with the antique furniture in the guest rooms.

"Maybe it's coming from outside," she said. "Would you like me to go take a look?"

Logan was about to reply when the hammering ceased. He waited.

"Mr. Walters?"

"Hang on." He waited a second longer. Nothing. He brought the receiver back to his ear. "No, that's okay. It stopped." Hopefully this time for good.

"Okay, then. Is there anything else I can do for you? I noticed you didn't come down for breakfast yet. Would you like something brought up?"

Logan glanced at the clock on the mantel of the old wood-burning fireplace: 8:26. He'd been awake since five, surviving on the in-room coffeemaker. His stomach growled. The offer was tempting, especially as the smell of fresh-baked pumpkin-spiced muffins filled the house. Scanning the messy room, he hesitated.

In less than twenty-four hours, he'd

made quite an impact on the small space. Clothes spilled out of his carry-on suitcase in front of the window. Yellow Post-it notes decorated the freshly painted dark blue walls above the desk, and his notebooks littered the floor, along with the homemade quilt thrown in a heap next to his damp towels. And the room still held the faintly nauseating smell of the Chinese takeout he'd ordered the night before.

"Um…no, thanks. I'll come down." After he restored the room to a livable state.

"Great, thank you. I have several guests checking in any minute, so I really shouldn't leave the desk until my partner, Victoria, arrives."

As Logan replaced the receiver, the sound of children squealing, running through the hallways made him wince. Spoke too soon about not hearing her children.

Coming here was a bad idea. He was never going to get any work done with the never-ending noise, in and outside the B & B. Being away from the distractions in the city was supposed to cure his writer's block. Alone in a place where he could focus on the story in progress and not the stack of personal issues that competed for his every thought.

He'd first discovered this small town when he lived in New Jersey, at the start of his writing career. Brookhollow had been a great weekend escape during his first novel. He'd hoped the inspiration he'd once found here might be waiting for him. He'd foolishly believed that things wouldn't have changed in the place in almost a decade.

Sitting at the desk, he stared at the open document on the screen. The idea of this sixth book—the final one in his mystery series—made him cringe. Halfway through, he realized his original idea of how to end the series that had defined his career and put him in the spotlight years before just wasn't good enough. His fans expected more and he didn't want to disappoint them.

He didn't have an alternative plan, either.

He scanned the last few paragraphs he'd written. The scene had stalled and he couldn't figure out why. He wondered if the point of view was the problem. Or maybe it was the setting? Something was definitely off. Maybe it was him. He needed to move on…come back to it later that evening. He worked better in the evening, anyway….

He flipped that page of his legal pad over and wrote “next scene” on the top of the next page, underlined it twice, then tapped his pen against the daunting blankness. If only he knew what the next scene was.

Out of the corner of his eye, he noticed the Dillon and McKay Law Office paperwork and reached for it. Leaning back in the chair, he scanned the letter from his ex-girlfriend’s lawyer for the millionth time. His vision blurred as it always did when he skimmed the third line. She was filing for full custody of Amelia Alexandra Kelland.

Full custody…and he’d get what? Visitation? No rights to make decisions about his little girl’s future?

He tossed the papers onto the desk.

If only they’d been married, he’d have had more rights. The thought of his ex-girlfriend made his blood boil and he forced himself to take a deep breath. She was moving to L.A. and wanted to take their daughter with her. He refused to let that happen.

The loud hammering resumed, and he dropped his pen as he stood. *That's it.* Grabbing his fleece jacket from the back of the antique rocking chair, he dashed out of the room, leaving the creaking old door to creep closed behind him. It would lock automatically, a lesson he'd learned the hard way the evening before. It had been two hours before the B & B owners returned from *dinner at a friend's.*

Taking the stairs two at a time toward the entryway, he collided with a petite blonde whose arms were full of shopping bags. The Brookhollow Inn's co-owner, Victoria Mason. She'd checked him in the day before.

"Good morning, Mr. Walters," she said, readjusting her load. "Something wrong?"

"Sorry, excuse me," he mumbled. Stopping in the entryway, he listened for the sound. Next door, to the right.

"Is everything okay?" Victoria called after him as he pushed the front door open.

"It will be once I get my hands on that hammer," Logan said as he stepped outside.

Several feet away he saw the source.

"What are you doing?" he asked, shielding his eyes from the glare of the early October sun. The woman next door, standing on a ladder in front of the house, wasn't the workman he'd been expecting, dressed as she was in a pair of tight black leggings and an oversize tan sweater. She wasn't wearing any shoes. "Hey!" he yelled when she didn't respond.

She turned abruptly at that, almost losing her footing on the ladder. "Whoa," she said, steadying herself. "Huh?"

"I said, what are you doing? Other than making a ton of noise." Logan studied the rickety ladder. Rusty and unstable, missing a rung in the center, the thing was a hazard.

"Hanging a sign," she answered, without looking at him.

"At this hour?"

"You're staying next door, right?" She paused, holding the sign against the house with one arm and gripping the roof for stability as she turned slightly to face him. Her long dark hair blew across her eyes, and she tucked it behind an ear.

"Yeah," he grumbled.

"Well, I have an agreement with the owners that I won't make any noise until after eight. It's almost nine and I'm almost done." She waved a hand, dismissing him.

"It's upside down."

"Seriously?" The woman sighed as she leaned back on the ladder to study her handy work. The ladder pulled away from the awning and she quickly leaned forward again. "Shoot." Turning the hammer around, she removed the last nail she'd driven in.

Logan scanned the sign, reading the upside-down words. "You're operating a day care next door to a bed-and-breakfast?" he asked through narrowed eyes. Just his luck. Not exactly ideal town planning in his opinion.

"Yeah. What's wrong with that?"

"I just think the bed-and-breakfast might lose business. . . ." He paused, his hands on his hips. "Although I guess what's the difference when there's already ten kids living in the house?"

This was no longer the place he remembered and definitely not the place for him to write. He'd get nothing done with children around, reminding him of how much he missed Amelia. Working from his home office, he'd been her primary caregiver—getting her ready for school in the morning, seeing her off to the bus and being there for after-school snacks while she did her homework before dinner. He loved every minute of being a father.

He needed to check out of here right away. Returning to his apartment, seeing Amelia's toys and her empty bedroom wouldn't be much better, but he couldn't stay.

"At the B-and-B? There are five children." The woman stretched to remove the nails on the other end of the sign. One foot left the ladder completely and Logan had to look away.

"There shouldn't be any. It's a business," he muttered, jamming his hands into his pockets and hunching deeper into his sweater. He shuffled his feet in the crunchy yellow and orange leaves on the sidewalk in front of her small bungalow.

"It's also a home." She flipped the sign around and lost her footing again on the ladder. She clutched the roof, struggling to regain her balance and reposition her stocking feet.

Stocking feet on an already unstable ladder? "Okay, that's it. Get down." Logan opened the gate of the white picket fence and moved toward her, motioning for her to descend the ladder.

"What?"

"Get...down!" he growled. "Give me the sign."

She hesitated.

He rattled the ladder.

"Fine, stop." She climbed down, stretching to reach the next rung below the missing one, then hesitated before handing over the sign. "You're not going to break it, are you?"

Logan grabbed the sign. The faster he could get this hung, the faster he could get back to work. Or at least back to staring at a blank page. Frowning, he climbed the wobbly ladder. "I can't believe I'm doing this."

"No one asked you." The woman folded her arms across her chest.

So much for gratitude, Logan thought as he paused halfway up the ladder. "Hey, is there supposed to be smoke inside your house?" Bending to peer through the window in the front of the house, he could see thick, dark clouds spiraling out of the oven toward the ceiling and, a second later, the smoke detector screeched.

"Smoke? No..." Her eyes widened. "My cookies." She lunged toward the door, threw it open and raced inside, oblivious that she'd just hit the ladder.

Oh no. Logan's arms flailed as the ladder fell away from the house, taking him with it, and crashed down on top of him on the cold ground. His arm hit the side of a rock-walled flower bed, and he cringed as pain seared his right wrist. His cheeks flamed hot, as he pushed the ladder off and sat up, rubbing the throbbing wrist. *Damn it.*

The woman came back outside, a frown wrinkling her forehead. "Well, the cookies are ruined," she said, tossing her hands up in the air and then shooting him a quizzical look as she took in the picture before her. "Did you fall?" She rushed to pick up the sign.

"No. You knocked me off."

Her mouth dropped open.

Logan grimaced as he tried to move his right hand. This was just great. The quickly swelling wrist ached with the slightest movement.

She knelt on the ground next to him. "Let me see your hand," she said, reaching for it.

At her touch he yanked his arm away. "Ow!"

"Ow? I hardly touched you."

"Well, don't." Logan levered himself up with his good hand and stood. He wanted to get as far away from her as possible.

When she scrambled to her feet, her eyes came level to his chest. "Fine." She took a step back and shoved several stray strands of hair away from her face to study his injury. "But you should get it looked at. It could be broken."

Broken? He groaned. A deep purple

bruise had already begun to spread across his hand. "I'm sure it's fine."

"I really don't think so. There's a medical clinic in town.... I have the children arriving soon, but if you want to wait until they all get here, I could drive you in the day-care van?"

That was a guilt offer if he'd ever heard one. Without even considering it, he shook his head. The medical clinic wasn't that far—he'd walk.

The woman pointed to the left. "Six blocks that way, take a right onto Main Street—"

"I know where it is."

"Oh...okay. You sure you don't want a ride? It's no trouble."

She was *not* a good liar.

"I'm sure."

She bent to get her sign. "Okay." Then picking up the ladder, she set it against the house.

"What are you doing?" Logan held his sore wrist with one hand.

"Hanging my sign," she said, stepping onto the first rung.

"Are you crazy? That ladder is a million years old."

A dark red minivan pulled up in front of the house, and she stepped down and waved, smiling warmly. The effect transformed her face as her dark eyes lit up and her features softened.

Logan's eyes followed hers to see two children climb out of the back of the van.

"Okay," he muttered, "well, thanks for the injury."

Holding up his purple, swollen hand, he went through the gate past the children and then the bed-and-breakfast, heading in the direction of the clinic.

"I DIDN'T REALIZE I was making so much noise over there with that sign, but he was pretty irate." Leigh took a sip of her chamomile tea from the oversize mug and curled a leg under her on the wicker chair, as she settled in the dining room of the bed-and-breakfast that evening. All day she'd been worried she might have caused trouble for her cousin Rachel and her partner, Victoria Mason...and she'd felt guilty about his injury. That swelling and bruising hadn't looked good. But she hadn't asked for his help. In fact, she never asked anyone for help. She'd learned the hard way that depending on someone else led to disappointment.

Rachel couldn't conceal her worry even as she said, "Ah, I didn't hear anything. He's just a grumpy guy.... Though he has been gone a long time," she added before biting into a raspberry muffin. "And yesterday, my kids drove him crazy running in the halls. It was raining so hard, I couldn't send them outside. Poor guy's not getting much peace and quiet with all the noise around here."

Leigh shook her head. "Kids playing is not noise, it's called fun."

"I don't know. My crew can be loud sometimes." She nodded toward the side of the yard where her older children used garden rakes to gather the leaves that had fallen from the oaks and maples in the spacious yard and piled them high.

"Looks like they're being helpful to me, cleaning up."

"Just wait."

A second later the three kids ran screaming, diving into the pile, rescattering leaves all over the yard.

"See?"

She couldn't help envying her cousin and her five children. After years of trying to have kids, she'd been unsuccessful. The problem wasn't conceiving. Three miscarriages, fertility treatments and countless tests had yet to determine the reason for her inability to carry a baby to term, and at thirty-eight, she was forced to face facts: having a child of her own wasn't a possibility.

Especially now that she found herself single again after ten years of marriage.

Neil had filed for divorce four years before, claiming that the stress of trying to have a family had taken its toll on their relationship and created a wedge between them that he couldn't get past.

Though she'd been devastated, she hadn't been able to argue with the obvious: their relationship had changed. She couldn't fault him for leaving. He wanted children and that wasn't something she could give him.

Rachel touched her hand, bringing her back to the present. She lowered her voice as she asked, "Have you heard from the adoption agency yet?"

The cousins were close, yet it still amazed Leigh how easily Rachel could read her thoughts. "They called last month to say they'd received the first portion of my deposit."

She toyed with the rim of the oversize mug. Deciding to adopt had been a major decision, and not one that she'd made lightly. She'd saved every cent of her divorce settlement from Neil for four years, waiting until she was certain she was ready to take this step, and now she was. She was fully prepared to raise a child on her own.

"It was enough to open my file and start the paperwork, but they said it could take months before I hear anything else." Her shoulders sagged. She knew this process wouldn't happen overnight, especially when she was hoping to adopt a newborn, but she was painfully aware that she wasn't getting any younger. She wanted to start a family before she turned forty.

"Don't worry, it will happen. You're terrific with the kids in your day care. Anyone can see you will make a wonderful mom someday." Rachel gave her hand a reassuring squeeze as Victoria joined them in the dining room, carrying a cup of black coffee.

"Sorry, I got caught up on the phone with Mrs. Dawson. She's planning a Halloween murder-mystery dinner at the recreation center and she wants to advertise the event in the *Brookhollow View*. I was helping her with the wording. What did I miss?"

Leigh shot her cousin a look. The only people she'd confided in about her adoption plans were Rachel and Grandmother Norris, and she wanted to keep the information between the three of them. Until she had a child of her own, she didn't want anyone to know she was going through the process. Disappointment was harder to bear when it had an audience, and if things didn't work out…

Victoria glanced between the two women and took a sip of her steaming coffee.

Rachel cleared her throat. "We were just

discussing our mysterious, brooding guest in the Blue Room."

"Mr. Walters?" Victoria's eyes narrowed. "He checked in yesterday morning. Said he planned to stay two or three weeks for sure, maybe longer. I checked out his website from the email address he left on file—he's some famous mystery novelist." She took another sip of coffee. "He almost knocked me off my feet when I came in today. What did he do now?"

"He was harassing Leigh about hanging her new day-care sign. Too loud." Rachel reached for the antique teapot on the table and refilled her cup.

"In fairness, he did try to help me with the sign." Leigh sighed. A writer? This was even worse than she'd thought. Was it too much to hope that he was left-handed? Though he probably required both hands to type.

"Then he fell off the ladder," Rachel struggled to say, her mouth full of raspberry muffin.

"Actually I opened my front door and knocked him off the ladder." Leigh hid sheepishly behind her tea mug, waiting for the reaction.

Victoria's eyes widened. "Is he okay?"

Leigh shrugged.

"Don't know," Rachel said. "I hope so. I haven't seen him since he rushed out of here this morning."

Victoria stared at Leigh. "I can't believe you."

Leigh ran her index finger around the mug. "I didn't mean to. I had cookies in the oven that were burning—"

Victoria waved that away. "I meant for using that old ladder. I told you not to use that rickety thing. It could have been *you* who fell. Please borrow ours anytime. Or better yet, just ask Luke to do it. He'd be happy to help," Victoria said, volunteering her husband's services.

The two had just gotten married in their second attempt at a wedding, after Victoria had called off the first one twelve years before when she moved to New York to follow her dream of a high-powered career. Luckily, fate had brought her home the previous Christmas and the two had realized their love had never faded, despite time and distance.

She bit a thumbnail. "Do you think he's okay? I'd hate to think one of our guests may have gotten hurt."

"I'm sure he's fine," Rachel said, but she didn't sound convinced.

The front door opened and a cool October breeze rustled the end of the tablecloth and paper napkins as Logan Walters entered his right hand in a plaster cast from wrist to elbow. His hard eyes zeroed in on Leigh.

She swallowed hard.

"Okay, maybe not." Rachel stood quickly and busied herself gathering their empty cups. She headed toward the kitchen.

"You." Scowling, he pointed a finger of his uninjured hand at Leigh.

"Me?" Leigh's eyes widened as she untucked her leg from beneath her on the chair and stood.

"Excuse me. I hear the phone ringing." Victoria dashed toward the front desk, leaving them alone.

Great, thanks, friends.

Logan stopped inches from her. His

height towered over her five-foot-two frame by almost a foot, but Leigh met his gaze.

"Look what you did." He held his cast close to her face.

So it *was* broken. No surprise there. "I said I was sorry, but no one asked you to climb that ladder." She sucked in her bottom lip. That hadn't come out right. She should have stopped at sorry.

He opened his mouth to speak, then shook his head. "This is what I get for helping," he muttered under his breath.

"I'm sorry. I'll pay your medical costs." The money in her emergency fund was dwindling and this would make a further dent in it, but it would be better than him suing her for getting hurt on her property. That possibility hadn't even occurred to her before now. She wondered if her homeowners' insurance covered something like this. Her day-care insurance covered the children in case of injury in her care, but another adult?

"I don't need your money. I have insurance," he grumbled, raking his casted hand through his hair. The sticky medical gauze got caught and he winced, pulling it free, taking with it several strands of dark brown hair. “Man, I can’t do anything with this thing on my hand.” Turning, he took quick, long strides out of the room.

She followed him into the hallway. “Mr. Walters, wait.”

He paused on the staircase, clearly exhausted.

“Is there anything I can do to help?” she asked, crossing her fingers behind her back. *Please say no.*

He hesitated, and she held her breath.

Shaking his head, he continued up the stairs. “No.”

LOGAN STRUGGLED TO position his hand on the desk, straining the fingers on his right hand to reach the keys on the laptop keyboard. The edge of the cast hit the space bar and he raised his arm, flinching in pain, and backspaced to where he’d left off typing. Flipping the page of his handwritten work, he tried to focus on something other than the pain in his arm. He could do this. He hit a few keystrokes and grimaced. With each letter, his wrist spasmed and pain rippled through his arm. The extra weight of the plaster cast made the muscles in his right shoulder ache.

Tossing the papers aside, he stood. How was he supposed to meet his editor's deadline like this? The writer's block had been bad enough; now he was physically incapable of getting the work done on time. Picking up his cell phone, he punched in his agent's number. The man had called him three times already today, and now there would be no more avoiding him.

"Clive Romanis," the man answered in his strong New York accent after the second ring.

"Clive, it's Logan."

"Hey, man, where are you? I've been calling you. You were supposed to email me those sample chapters two days ago."

Logan cringed. The promised chapters hadn't been written yet. Another reason he'd had to leave the city. It was easier to avoid his agent when he wasn't living two blocks from his office. "Yeah, sorry, I left the city for a while to clear my head, get this book finished."

"What do you mean you left the city?

Where did you go?" The man's voice barely contained his disbelief. Clive wasn't truly convinced that there was anything beyond the New York City limits.

"Just a small town in New Jersey. I wrote part of the first book out here. It's quiet and peaceful," he lied.

It used to be.

"New Jersey?"

"Yes."

Clive released a deep breath. "Tell me this isn't you running away from your commitments."

"No, of course not." Running away and needing to get away for a while were two different things, weren't they?

"So you're writing? You're getting it done?"

"Yeah.... Look, I've run into a bit of a problem meeting the deadline." His best bet would be to pack up, head back to New York and hire a typist. The thought made him uneasy. He never let anyone read his work before it was done, especially a stranger. Other than his agent and his editor, he never discussed plotlines with anyone. And with the comeback he was making, he couldn't chance that the resolution of years of work would be leaked before the book even hit the shelves.

"Logan, we've pushed the deadline back twice now. If I ask for another extension from the publisher, they may postpone the release dates."

Logan pushed the covers aside and sat on the edge of the bed. "That's ridiculous." So he'd had a few years of a dry spell after the fourth book. He'd delivered book five to them on time. Book six was almost done. Sort of. If he could just figure out a conclusion.

"They're nervous that you're going to flake on them again. Truthfully, I'm not sure you won't, either. I've pulled all the strings I can, Logan. If you don't have the book on my desk in three weeks, they won't release book five next month. You're lucky your readers haven't given up hope on you yet."

"I broke my right hand," Logan said with a sigh as he stood and paced the room again.

"Nice try, Logan." His agent sounded discouraged. "Now I've heard it all from you. If you call me next week and say your dog ate the final draft, I'm walking."

"Seriously, I broke it. It's in a plaster cast and it's useless." Logan sat in the wooden rocking chair near the window, the painkillers they'd given him at the clinic, making him drowsy but not doing much for the pain. Closing his eyes, he leaned his head against the back of the chair.

"How far along are you?" Panic had crept into the older man's voice.

Logan hesitated. If he told the truth, that he no longer had any idea where the plot was heading or how to end the entire series, the man might drop him as a client. "Far enough from the end that I can't possibly type it all with only one good hand in three weeks."

Clive let out a deep, slow breath. "Okay. This sucks, but we can still meet the deadline. Why don't you check out that voice-recognition software? Some of my other clients use it and love it."

"Uh-uh, forget it. The thoughts just don't seem to flow that way. Besides, I doubt there's a store nearby that would carry it, and ordering it could take a few days."

"Well, get your butt back to the city and I'll call a typing service. I'm sure they can have someone available within twenty-four hours."

"I'm really not comfortable with that idea."

"Now is not the time for your paranoia. Those people don't even read, they just type." Clive's voice rose. "For that matter, Logan, I'll come type it for you myself."

The last thing he needed was the one person in his life who still believed in his talent to give up on him. He had to get this book finished. "No. I'll think of something. I'll get it done." Logan rubbed his aching forehead with his good hand and stood.

"I need the finished manuscript on my desk by November fifth."

"You'll have it." Logan disconnected the call and tossed his cell phone onto the bed. Walking to the window, he drew back the thick lace curtains for the first time. Through the fall leaves of the maple in the yard, he could see the day care lady next door, removing the children's blankets from the clothesline.

He watched as she folded the blankets and laid them neatly in the basket.

She didn't seem like someone who would rush to the media with the book's ending. She probably hadn't even heard of him.

As she put the plastic cover on the outdoor sandbox, he couldn't help wondering about her. In the few days he'd been there, today had been the first he'd even noticed anyone next door. Years ago, he remembered the place being vacant. Now that the day care kids were gone, he didn't see anyone else around—no husband? No kids?

His phone chimed and reaching for it, he read the text message from Clive. *I need you to get this done.*

Going back to the window, he scanned the yard next door, but she'd already gone back inside.

He hesitated. If he went back to the city now, Clive would be riding him for the next three weeks. The media and reviewers were already starting to hound him for interviews since the press release announcing the new book was sent out the month before. And being in his apartment without his daughter and worrying about her in California would be torture. He'd left the city for those reasons and they would be waiting for him when he went back.

He didn't like any of his options, but asking the strange woman next door for help was probably the one he hated the least.

I've figured out a way, he texted back.

POURING A CUP of steaming apple cider into her favorite mug and grabbing a new romance novel from the counter, Leigh did a final scan of the kitchen. The high chairs were sanitized and set up for breakfast in the morning. Plastic plates and sippy cups sat drying in the rack on the counter, and the painting easel was set up with new finger paints and paper. Turning off the kitchen light, she carried her cider and book to the sitting area in the front of her house. The glass sunroom with the comfy rocking chair and ottoman and the bookshelf lining one wall was her favorite spot, especially in winter when she lit the fireplace. Fluffing a pillow behind her, she sat and opened her book to the bookmark. She scanned the page, rereading several pages. Ah…right…the scene where the hero and heroine finally acknowledge their feelings. Always her favorite part in a romance. Romances were supposed to make impossible situations work, and this one didn't fail to deliver. If only real life were that way. She took a sip of her cider and snuggled deeper into her cardigan.

A few minutes later, a loud thud on the front door made her jump, spilling the hot liquid. She wiped at the wet spots on her dark leggings and oversize sweater, and set the book aside.

Another loud knock on her door made her rush to the entranceway. One of the kids' parents? She didn't recall finding any items left behind.

She stood on tiptoe and glanced through the peephole on the door as she unlocked the dead bolt, which seemed like overkill in Brookhollow but served to keep the children from getting out into the front yard.

Mr. Walters paced the front porch, his

head down against the wind. What was he doing here? Come to yell at her some more? Serve her with a lawsuit for getting injured on her property? She opened the door with a sigh and placed a hand on her hip. "Look, I've already apologized—"

"I need your help," he mumbled.

"Huh?" She hid her body behind the door, the cool air making her shiver. "With what?" she asked suspiciously.

"Typing." He held up his broken hand.

She stared at him, trying to process his request. Finally she said, "I know I offered to help you, but the truth is...I can't type."

It was his turn to stare at her.

She shrugged helplessly. She'd never bothered to learn. She rarely used a computer. Had no real need for it, except to email or chat with her parents who were on one of their mission trips. All of her friends were within a stone's throw of her house, so she didn't need social media to reach them. Other than those weekly sessions with her parents, her computer sat untouched in the den. Surely, Logan needed someone more computer literate.

After several beats he said, "You have

two operational hands. Anything you do will be better than what I'm capable of."

"Don't they have services that provide that kind of help for writers?" she asked, biting her lip. She'd been hoping to avoid him for the duration of his stay. She'd assumed he wouldn't be in a rush to see her anytime soon, either.

"I wouldn't need help if I hadn't broken my wrist…helping you."

"Well, I…" Leigh shifted from one leg to the other. *Crap, crap, double crap.* She knew she had to help—she had offered after all, but…

"I'll pay you." She heard his cool, distant desperation. The sound of a man hating the words coming out of his own mouth.

She hesitated, searching for a way out of this. Sure, she felt guilty, but since her divorce…she just didn't want to spend time with a man this good-looking. Or any man, really. Didn't want any possibility of romantic entanglements in her near future. "I don't know when I'll have time. I have the kids every day, during the day—well, Monday to Friday at least."

Logan grimaced.

"Yes, I know how you feel about children," Leigh said, rolling her eyes. Heartless man. Who didn't love children? Most men her age were looking to settle down, have a family. Which was why she found herself single at thirty-eight.

Everyone in town knew about her inability to have a child.

The fact that everybody knew her personal failure—the one loss in her life she still grieved almost every minute of every day—was the only aspect of living in Brookhollow she didn't like.

She didn't blame the men for keeping their distance, though. Her own husband hadn't been able to deal with her infertility.

"What about evenings?" he said.

Evenings. Her alone time…her books…her bubble baths…

"Please, Leigh."

Exhaling slowly, she said, "Okay." She would regret this. She just knew it.

"Thank you." The words were choked out. Clearly, he didn't use them often.

Opening the door a little wider, she said, "The kids are usually gone by five-thirty, so if you want to come over around six."

Logan shook his head. “I was hoping we could work at the bed-and-breakfast. My stuff is scattered all over the place.” He paused when he registered her reluctance. “What?”

“You’re not from a small town, are you?”

“What do you mean?”

“I can’t come over to your room at the bed-and-breakfast every night. Rumors would spread through town so fast.” Rumors kept Brookhollow alive with excitement.

Logan frowned. “Who cares what people think?”

“I do. You get to leave once your book is done.” She lowered her voice, “But I—” she pointed to herself “—live here.” Folding her arms, she said, “No way. In fact, my place isn’t really an option, either.” A handsome stranger entering her house every night…she could only imagine what her grandmother Norris would have to say if she found out.

For too long her life had been the topic of conversation in the local diner, beauty salon and just about anywhere people congregated in town.

"Well, where?"

Leigh considered the options. If he was trying to keep a low profile around town, there weren't many. Finally she said, "How about the gazebo in the backyard of the bed-and-breakfast? It's heated, with a picnic table and lighting, and it's secluded enough in the back corner of the yard near all the big trees that no one will notice."

"Outside?"

"Yes."

"It's October. It's absolutely freezing once the sun sets." Logan shivered to prove his point. "Isn't there a library or something?"

"Just about everything closes around here at six. Besides, if you want to keep your presence quiet—a public place isn't really going to work, is it?" She waited. If he wanted her help, they did it her way or not at all. She didn't need anything or anyone complicating her life.

Logan let out a deep breath. "Okay, fine." He stared down at his offending wrist, weighted down as it must have been by the plaster, and turned to leave. "Tomorrow at six in the gazebo."

Wonderful. She prayed his book was almost finished. "Can't wait."

"Lying really isn't your thing," he called over his shoulder.

CHAPTER TWO

THE NEXT MORNING, Logan hesitated before opening the email from his lawyer, Eric James. The Manhattan Family Law Group didn't waste time or their client's money emailing without a good reason. Lately, whenever he heard from them, it was bad news, and he wasn't sure he could handle the stress that morning. His hand and wrist throbbed, and the painkillers they'd prescribed at the clinic didn't seem to help.

The message was marked urgent. There was no avoiding it. Opening it, he scanned it quickly.

Kendra's lawyer had requested a financial statement. Fantastic. He had known that sooner or later she would play that card. Supporting his daughter with his writing was possible, given his investments and the royalties from his upcoming release, but his lawyer had cautioned him that proving his income in court might be challenging. Self-employed parents without medical benefits had a tougher time convincing the judge they could offer the best support.

Another reason he had to finish this book. Frustrated, he stood. The issues in his personal life were driving him to distraction and preventing him from writing, yet if he didn't write, things in his personal life would be even worse. Without a steady income, no judge would award him custody of Amelia.

Lying on the bed, he closed his eyes, fighting to control the desperation and hopelessness he couldn't escape.

Hours later, he sat on the wooden bench under the shelter of the gazebo. The October setting sun cast a glare across his laptop screen as he readjusted the computer into the shade. At least it wasn't cold inside the heated space. Checking his watch, he stood: 5:58. Where was she?

He checked his watch again. Still 5:58. Time honestly passed slower in this small town, he was convinced of it. Two days before, that had been part of its original appeal; not anymore. He sat back down on the bench.

The sound of crunching leaves caught his attention. In the dusk, he saw Leigh—in a pair of baggy, faded jeans and a T-shirt with a sweater thrown over her shoulders—carrying a brown wicker basket. She smiled wearily as she approached.

She looked about as excited to do this as he was. He moved some of his papers aside to make room for the basket.

"I brought some snacks, in case," she said, sliding her arms into her sweater and tugging it down over her head.

"I'm not hungry…thanks." He opened his notebook to the pages to be transcribed. "So, here is where I left off typing." He pointed to the middle of the page and moved the mouse to bring up the document.

Leigh busied herself with the basket, taking out a Thermos and pouring coffee into a mug. She took out a raspberry muffin and a plastic container of butter, then napkins and plastic cutlery. And then…a fruit tray?

"What are you doing?" Logan asked.

"I haven't eaten dinner yet." She bit into her muffin. "Mmm.... I got them from my grandmother's bakery when I took the kids on an afternoon walk. She owns Ginger Snaps...."

He was barely listening, hearing an overbearing ticking in his brain as the sun continued to set.

"Are you sure you don't—"

"I'm sure," Logan snapped. He raked his left hand through his hair and rubbed his four-day-old beard.

Leigh frowned, took another quick bite of the muffin and turned her attention to his notebook. "Okay, sorry. I'm listening. So, these are your notes." She squinted, leaning closer to the scribbled writing on the yellow legal pad.

"No, this is the first draft of the book," Logan said, betraying his exasperation. He hated to be sharing this with anyone. The first draft was always written in haste, without care to grammar and punctuation. Sometimes he skipped over names. Not exactly a polished, finished product.

"And you wrote this before you broke your hand?"

Logan looked at the tiny chicken scratches. So they were hard to read. "That's why we need to do this together. I'll read it as you type." He picked up the pad of paper and gestured for Leigh to take a seat in front of the laptop. "Ready?"

"Okay, go." Her hands poised midair, she waited. "Go slowly, I wasn't lying when I said I can't type."

Logan cleared his throat and opened his mouth. Nothing came out.... Reading his own unedited passages to her would be pure torture. He would find something wrong with each line. He usually did a round of editing as he transcribed.

Leigh turned to him. "You can't read your writing, either?"

Logan tossed the pad back onto the table. "This isn't going to work."

Leigh held her hands up. "I'm sorry, I won't make any more jokes." She popped a chunk of muffin into her mouth and poised her hands over the keys. "Ready," she said, her mouth full, a crumb falling onto the keys.

Sliding the laptop away from her, Logan picked it up and closed the lid. “Never mind,” he said as he unzipped his laptop case and shoved the computer inside.

“I don’t understand.” Leigh stared up at him. “I thought you needed help.”

He gathered his notes. “I do, but…” He paused as he stood. “You wouldn’t understand.”

“You’re probably right, but now I just think you’re a little crazy, so…”

The look on her face indicated she did indeed think he was crazy and he laughed, surprising himself.

And her. Her mouth dropped but to her credit, she recovered quickly. “Nice to see you’re actually capable of a smile,” she said, moving over on the bench to make room for him. She picked up her coffee and took a sip.

Reluctantly, he sat. “The thing is…I never let people read my work until it’s done.”

“Yes, you mentioned that.”

“And this book is unique in that it’s the last book in a series.” Did she know who he was? "The Van Gardener series." He paused, waited.

She blinked. No recognition showed on her face, which he couldn't help noticing was flawless in the glow of the setting sun.

"You don't know it?" Could he really had stumbled upon one of the few people who hadn't heard about the series, or his inability to finish it? One of the few who hadn't read the extensive media coverage about his separation and his custody battle for Amelia...or the articles speculating he'd dropped off the map because of alcohol and/or drug addictions?

"No, I'm sorry if I should. I am an avid reader...I'm just not into suspense-filled mysteries." She shuddered.

The tension of the past twenty-four hours eased a little. It was nice to meet someone with no preconceived opinions about him. "I guess it's not really the kind of book you read to preschoolers," he said, wiggling his fingers inside the cast.

"Itchy?" Leigh gestured toward the cast. "Every summer at least one of my kids—my day-care kids, I mean—breaks something or other. Thankfully not under my watch," she added, reaching for a plastic fork. "Here, try this." She handed it to him.

He took it and slid it into the cast. Instant relief. "Ah..."

"Better?"

"Much." He tried to hand her back the fork.

She grimaced. "Keep it."

He laughed again. Wow, twice in five minutes, more than he'd laughed in months.

"So, are we going to do this, given that I have no idea who you are or anything about the series?" Leigh waited, watching him over the rim of her coffee cup.

Logan hesitated. She had the most trustworthy face; her sincerity and genuine nature shone in her eyes. Probably why she was so great with children. Children could distinguish real honesty and affection.

Leigh checked her watch. "We're wasting time," she said, "and I have more muffins."

"Okay. But I need you to sign something." Tearing out a piece of paper, he glanced from it to his left hand. She'd have to write their agreement. He held out his silver monogrammed pen, his favorite, the only one he ever used. "I need you to write that you won't reveal the contents of this book to anyone."

She took the pen and wrote.

He watched in silence.

She paused and glanced toward him. "Anything else?"

That pretty much captured what he needed from her in a nutshell. "Just sign and date it, please."

Leigh did as he asked and handed it back. "This book is a big deal, huh?"

He used to think so. The series had dominated his every waking thought for seven years, losing him his one and only serious relationship, his friendships and his sanity. Now he just wanted to finish it, dig himself out from the shadow of doubt and regain confidence in his abilities as a writer, in his own eyes as well as those of the court that would be deciding his and his daughter's fate. "Yeah, it's a big deal."

TWO DAYS LATER, Leigh peered around the corner of Main Street. The town's leasing office was above the bank and she was desperate to avoid her ex-husband's new wife, Angela Conway, one of the only real-estate agents in town.

Living in the same town with the couple and their two young children was tough, and Angela's office was two doors down from Leigh's grandmother's bakery. It wasn't that she didn't like the woman, and she wasn't jealous of the life she and Neil shared with the family she hadn't been able to give him…of course not.

Logan was right, she really wasn't good at lying, not even to herself.

As she moved quickly past the brick office building, she waved to Kimberley Mitchell, one of the bank-loans officers, staring out her ground-floor office window with her phone cradled to her shoulder. Then, head down, eyes glued to the brick-patterned sidewalk, Leigh continued on, pretending not to hear Angela's voice as she called from a window overhead.

She paused for effect when she heard the second, louder "Leigh!", glancing in every direction but the one she knew the sound was coming from and then continued in a hurry. She heard her call again, but this time she dove around the side of Pearl's Petals, the flower shop on the corner across from her grandmother's bakery.

How was she going to get across the street without Angela seeing her? A quick glance revealed she was still waiting at the open window. She ducked her head back around the corner.

"Who are we hiding from?" a man whispered inches from her right ear.

Leigh jumped, her hand flying to her chest, knocking over a row of small potted plants on the outside sale table display at Pearl's.

Logan dove for one pot before it fell off the table. He caught it easily in his left hand and set it back carefully, straightening the others and brushing the scattered leaves and dirt off the white tablecloth.

"Thanks," Leigh said. She would've hated to have to buy all of those plants if she'd broken them. Children were her area of expertise—plants not so much. "And I'm not hiding," she said, but she suspected her flaming cheeks gave her away. Gingerly, she touched the leaves on a plant she'd never be able to name if asked. "I'm shopping." Pretending to be interested in one, she picked it up and examined it.

"Get many cuts and burns?"

"No. Why?" she asked, casting him a puzzled look.

"That's an aloe plant," Logan explained. "Shouldn't you have an entourage of kids?"

"A college student works with me part-time. She's doing a practicum for her childhood-education certificate. Gives me time to run errands." She poked her head around the corner quickly. Angela was still there.

Logan leaned around the corner. "Okay, tell me where I'm supposed to be looking."

"I don't know what you're talking about."

"You better tell me, or I'll blow your cover."

"Fine," Leigh snapped. "Last building on the corner, upstairs window." She waited, hands on her hips, ignoring the plants.

"All clear," Logan said.

Leigh let out a sigh of relief and stepped away from the shelter of the building.

"Why are you hiding from someone?"

She read the amusement in his dark eyes as he studied her. “I’m not, really,” she said with a shrug, as she moved around him, checking both ways before crossing Main Street.

Logan followed. “Okay, fine…let’s see.” He paused, appearing to think. “I know, it’s an angry day-care dad looking for a tax receipt. No, wait, it’s someone suing you for that hazardous front porch step of yours.”

“There’s nothing wrong with your creative juices now.”

“I can keep guessing, I’ve got all day. I should be writing, but someone pushed me off a ladder.”

“Okay,” Leigh said, holding her hands up in defeat as he matched his step to hers. “It’s my ex-husband’s new wife.”

He stumbled and paused to get his balance before keeping up with her again. “Wouldn’t have guessed that one.”

“Can I point you in any certain direction, Mr. Walters?” She refused to elaborate, despite the intense curiosity written all over his handsome face. At least curiosity softened the sharp edges of this man she'd only known for a few days.

"I don't know. Where are you headed?"

Leigh thought fast. "The gynecologist."

Logan smiled.

Huh, dimples—hadn't noticed them before. They should make an appearance more often, she thought.

"You're getting better with the lies. I'll catch you later. Same time, gazebo?"

"Sure thing."

She watched as he dashed off down the block before heading in the opposite direction.

Moments later Leigh stepped into Dog Eared Books. It was discouraging to see the going-out-of-business sale posters in the window behind their annual Halloween decor of orange lights and pumpkins carved in the images of bestselling books. The bookstore had been in Brookhollow for over fifty years. Grandma Norris had taken her there for the first time on her fourth birthday, when she and her parents had stayed longer than usual after the holidays. She'd filled almost another full suitcase full of books for her trip overseas to the new mission her dad had been appointed to, and they had been such a comfort—she remembered that clearly even though she'd only been four years old.

As a teenager, after her parents sent her to live with her grandmother to attend Brookhollow High, she'd visited the store almost every day, spending the money she earned from her part-time summer job at the Theatre Under the Stars drive-in.

"Hello," she said, stepping over boxes of books in the entryway. She would miss the landmark once the store closed in the new year.

Danielle O'Connor came from the back storage room, another box of books in her arms. "Hi, Leigh. Sorry for the mess. Just trying to reorganize some things."

Leigh scanned the labels on the boxes near the wall. "Those are books for the library?"

"Yeah, they're all fairly new—novels released this year. There are some children's books in there, as well. You're welcome to take a look."

"Thank you, but trust me, I'm running out of space for more books."

"That's not possible," Danielle said. "You just have to build higher shelves." She gestured to the floor-to-ceiling bookshelves along the first floor of the two-story space."

"I guess so," Leigh said with a laugh. "Anyway, I did stop by for a couple of specific novels. Do you think you could search your database to see if you have them? They're seven or eight years old. If they're already packed away, don't worry."

Danielle moved to the other side of the counter to her computer. "Romance?" she asked with a knowing smile.

"Actually no…um…mystery?"

"You—mystery?" Danielle raised an eyebrow.

Leigh shrugged. "Thought I'd broaden my horizons a little."

Daniel shook her head slowly as she clicked on the mystery tab and they waited for the page to load. "Name of the book?"

"*Danger Within* by…um…Logan Walters." She wondered if somehow news had already spread through town about Logan's visit.

If Danielle had heard, she didn't reveal

it. "Here it is…part of the Van Gardener series, right?"

"That's it. Do you have the complete set?"

"Yes, as a matter of fact, I just put them on the fifty-cent table outside."

Leigh suppressed a cringe. Logan would certainly take a blow to his ego if he knew the first four books of his popular series were reduced to the quick-sale bargain table.

If he found out she bought them, she'd claim she'd spent at least a dollar on them.

"Great, I'll take them all."

THIS TOWN really had changed a lot since the last time he was here, Logan thought as he left the sports museum, Legend's, with a signed NFL jersey he'd paid a premium for. Most of the items in the museum were rare collectables, things that used to belong to Don Jamieson, the late NFL quarterback who used to own Legend's when it was a sporting-goods store. Logan wasn't that into sports, but he knew his agent would love the signed jersey. He owed the man a good Christmas gift after the headache of a year they'd suffered.

As he turned the corner of Main Street and Commerce Avenue, he came to a halt as a long line of children getting off a school bus blocked his path.

The young schoolteacher smiled. "Sorry, we're almost at the end of them," she said, continuing to check off her list of students as they went past, up the stairs to the... Logan glanced at the building, shielding his eyes from the midmorning sun. Library. At three stories, it was by far one of the largest buildings in Brookhollow.

"No problem. Field trip?" he asked.

"Yes, sort of. It's literacy week, so we're here to listen to today's readers."

Literacy week. That's right, in New York every year he donated proceeds from his book sales to this great cause. He'd credit books with helping him find his own future path, often providing an escape and hope that was rare in the harsh reality of his foster-care situations. As the last child passed, Logan followed the teacher up the stairs. In truth, though New York was home to one of the country's most beautiful libraries, he hadn't been inside one in years. Maybe it would help with the writer's block. "I think I'll check it out myself. Thank you, Miss...?"

"Ally. Miss Ally." With a wave, she disappeared after the children inside.

Pausing at the top of the steps, Logan took a moment to read the literacy-week schedule posted on a sign on the door. Readings for children and adults...book discussion groups...a book sale that weekend. All the same events hosted by the big-city libraries. Without the crowds, he speculated, as he entered the building.

Two school groups were gathered in a reading room to the right of the main entrance. He could tell they were two different groups by the colored uniforms they wore. The sight of the smaller ones in their navy smocks and tights reminded him of his daughter. Amelia, eight, attended a private school in New York, one of the few that still insisted on a dress-code uniform.

Amelia.

He missed his little girl so much. She would have loved a school outing like this. Her favorite subject was English. Liked to make up stories…some of which he'd illustrated for her. He had those stories saved in the top drawer of his writing desk in his apartment in Manhattan, one of the few things he'd taken from the home he'd shared with Kendra when he moved out two years before.

Two years.

Some days it felt as if they'd been battling in court over the separation and custody forever, and other days it felt like no time at all. He just hoped they reached a conclusion next month. He couldn't take much more of this.

His weekly phone call to California to speak to his kid was hardly enough, but with the time difference and his daughter's need to adjust to her new surroundings, he was biting his tongue and giving them space. He didn't want to make things harder on Amelia. But next month, regardless of the outcome of the custody case, things had to change. He deserved and wanted more time with his daughter.

He stepped into the library.

To his relief, it looked pretty much like he'd expected it to, which was soothing to his frayed, blocked nerves. Big city or small, there was comfort in the familiarity of the rows of shelves and the smell of books.

To his right was a children's section, complete with a puppet theater. But the focal point was a floor-to-ceiling plastic oak tree with the alphabet in its leaves, benches around its trunk and books stashed in the bark.

A librarian reshelving books asked, "Can I… Oh my God." Several browsers on the other side of the shelf turned to look at them.

"Hi," he said.

"You're Logan Walters." The woman, not old but older than him, stood.

"Yes, I am." He extended his good hand to her.

She stared at him, wide eyes, mouth agape, not moving.

Maybe he should have said no, he thought when she continued to stare. Uncomfortable, he shifted from one leg to the other. Then he dropped the hand he'd extended. "You okay?"

"Yes…this is incredible," she said, finding her voice. "I'm sorry, I just wasn't expecting... I mean no one told me you were coming. That's the mayor's office for you. They forget to tell us everything. Although maybe they wanted to surprise me—that was nice of them." Her face lit up in a wide smile and she readjusted her thick, red-rimmed glasses higher on her nose and tucked a few strands of strawberry blond hair behind an ear. The unruly wisps just bounced right back toward her cheek.

Cute.

"Actually no one sent me. I'm staying at the Brookhollow Inn, working on a book." Duh. He shouldn't have said that. Guess his plan to stay here unnoticed was out the window.

"Oh, sorry, I thought since it was literacy week... We sometimes bring in guest authors, though no one as famous as you." Her open admiration made him a little shy.

It had been years since he'd encountered a fan; mainly because he'd reclusively avoided all opportunities to meet them. But also because he hadn't published a book in so long. *Out of sight, out of mind* was usually the case in this industry. Guess Clive had been right about the diehards standing by, waiting for his final book.

He just hoped he could deliver what his fans expected and deserved. "I seemed to have got caught up in the wake of all these kids coming into the library and was swept in myself.... Kids are quite a force of nature," he added lamely, losing the calm the library had given him in his returning panic over the writer's block.

"Well, it's certainly a pleasure to meet you. I'm Kate Richardson." She extended her right hand, but for the first time noticed his in a cast and quickly switched to the left one for a clumsy welcome. "That looks like a new cast. What happened?"

"Broke my wrist."

"How?"

"Trying to help someone a couple of days ago."

She nodded. "As they say, no good deed goes unpunished."

"I guess not."

"Gotta be tough to get any writing done like that." Her smile was sympathetic.

He didn't want to tell her that the break gave him a more plausible excuse for the lack of productivity that was driving him insane, so he just nodded. "Quiet day?"

"Well, e-books have really made a dent in our clientele." But she shook her head. "Not quiet today with two loads of schoolkids for literacy week. The kids who swept you in here?" she reminded him, tilting her head to the reading room across the foyer.

"Ah, yes, literacy week."

"As for me," she added, "I like my books—real books. The ones you can touch, smell, hug..." Her cheeks flushed.

"Hug?"

"Only the really great ones. Speaking of which..." She nodded toward the next aisle.

Logan followed her.

"Here are yours." She waved at the four books lining the shelf, numbered and tagged with the Brookhollow Library category logo. "I've read them all, twice." The admiration was back in her eyes. "I just love Van and Piper."

The detective partners in his books were essentially the main characters, though the series was titled for Van. Piper Kelly was more or less Van's sidekick and Logan had only introduced her midway through the second book, under the guidance of the publisher. Adding in the coed working relationship was supposed to increase his female readership. "Thank you. I'm glad you enjoyed them."

"Very much." Her hand suddenly went to the pen behind her ear. "Hey, would you sign them?"

He glanced at the cast on his hand. "As soon as the swelling goes down and I can hold a pen a little better, sure. I'll stop by again before I leave town."

"Great. Oh, excuse me for a second." She went to help a petite blonde waiting at the information desk, and as Logan perused the shelves, he could feel two sets of eyes watching him. By ten everyone would know he was there. Why had he given out his address?

"Um, Mr. Walters?" Kate called a moment later.

Barely suppressing a groan, reluctantly he walked over to the desk where the librarian gestured toward the other woman, who was holding a stack of novels. “Hi,” he muttered, struggling to be gracious.

“Hi. I’m Randi Carter, the principal of Brookhollow High,” she said.

Crap, he felt a favor coming next.... He waited for it, hoping he was wrong. “Kate was just telling me that you’re a bestselling mystery writer. I apologize—I barely have time to read for pleasure and I’m unfamiliar with your work.” She followed his gaze down to the books in her arms. “These are for the homeroom classes.”

“I haven’t produced anything in a while actually, so...”

“Will you be in town long?” she asked.

He hesitated. But then thought, he’d pretty much already blown his cover, anyway. Giving away more of his coveted private information couldn’t hurt. “A few weeks.” His original goal had been two. Now he hoped he could make his deadline, which was a little over three weeks away.

“Great. Well, what we were just discussing, and wondering, is if you might be available to do a school visit while you were here?”

And there it was. “A school visit?”

"Yes, for my grade-twelve creative-writing class."

He looked from her back to Kate, the librarian, who was nodding her encouragement. "You want me to come talk to the students?"

"If you could. We rarely…okay, never… have your caliber of writing talent in Brookhollow and there are a few students in that class that show real promise. I think getting to meet you would be a great honor for them, and any knowledge you can impart to them would be greatly appreciated."

"Oh…um…" Coming here to avoid reminders of how much he missed Amelia had certainly backfired. There were children everywhere—more children than adults in Brookhollow. The B & B and the day care next door were unavoidable, but purposely going into the school? He'd have to be crazy.

"Only if you have time, of course," Kate said, earning a frown and a *shhh* from Randi.

Both women were staring at him expectantly. As if he should be excited to do his duty by the local school and support such a worthy cause. Sure, at seventeen he would have killed for this kind of opportunity. But now… These two didn't understand that he had three weeks to write this book, finish the series that had made his name. Find a way to support his child and win back custody. Three weeks.

Why wouldn't they stop staring at him?

Finally, slowly, he said, "I'll be there," wondering how he could possibly agree to this and still get what he wanted—*needed*—and leave Brookhollow in just three weeks

Three weeks.

"LOGAN, WHAT DOES THIS say?" Leigh squinted at the smeared scribbled ink on the back of a tiny ripped piece of napkin, stuffed among the pages of notes. She turned it over in her hands. "Isn't this from Jack in the Box?"

"Inspiration always hits when I don't have a real piece of paper," he replied. "Let me see." They were sitting side by side on the bench inside the—thankfully heated—gazebo that evening. They were making progress, and the night before they'd managed to get through the remaining handwritten notes he'd left to type in. During the day, he'd worked on more content, as well as he could. "Oh, this was new dialogue I'd thought of to add to scene three in chapter four. Thanks, I was looking for this."

She suspected he'd forgotten he'd even written it, but she kept the thought to herself.

Taking the laptop from her, Logan scrolled back to find the spot in the fourth chapter. Then he slid the laptop back to her. "I'll read it to you."

"Okay, go." Leigh popped a piece of lemon-poppy-seed muffin into her mouth and got ready to type. She turned to look at him when he remained silent. "What?"

"How are you not two hundred pounds eating all of these muffins?" He stared at her. "I mean every night we work together, you consume, like, half a dozen."

She arched an eyebrow.

He held his hands up. "I'm not saying there's anything wrong with it.... It just amazes me. You must have an incredible metabolism."

Hmm…maybe she should allow him to think she was one of those lucky people who could eat anything they wanted without gaining weight. Instead she said, "It's my grandma's secret ingredient."

"Which is?"

"I can't reveal it," she said through another mouthful.

"Who am I going to tell? Seriously, do I look like I'm going to run out and open a competing bakery in Brookhollow?"

She studied him. "Maybe I should make you sign something."

"Ha." He rolled his eyes. "Funny lady."

Leigh coughed on crumbs as she suppressed a laugh. "It's protein powder…. Plus she uses a sugar substitute." She pushed the basket at him.

He reached inside and took one. He hesitated, examining it. He sniffed it. "I can't believe you didn't tell me these were healthy to eat before now," he said through a mouthful.

"Excuse me, I hadn't realized you were trying to keep your boyish physique."

Now it was his turn to choke on his muffin. "Okay, let's continue," he managed to say.

"Ready."

He remained silent behind her.

"What now? Time's wasting."

"I know, I just noticed how small your hands are. No wonder you type so slow. Can you even reach all the keys?"

Leigh glanced at him, eyebrow raised yet again. "Are we typing or not?"

"Sorry. Okay, so the first line of dialogue is, 'Don't go down there.'"

"Wait," she interrupted.

"What?"

"Who's saying this?"

"The detective."

She frowned and pursed her lips.

"What?"

She hesitated, then shook her head. This was his book. "Nothing," she said, typing in the dialogue.

Logan held a hand out to stop her. "No, really, what?" He frowned, studying the words on the page.

Leigh sighed. "Okay, it's just that it doesn't make sense."

"What doesn't make sense?"

"That the detective would say, 'Don't go down there.' It's kind of like telling a child, 'Don't look in the cupboard for a cookie.' Of course they're going to do it now, even if they hadn't planned to."

"Exactly," Logan said with a nod.

"You want the bad guy to go downstairs? But in the next scene, that doesn't work in the detective's favor."

"Not in that scene, but eventually it will." Logan reached for his notes and flipped ahead. "See, here." He pointed to a scribbled paragraph, written diagonally across a length of cash register receipt.

"Is this from the grocery store?" Leigh picked it up and turned it over.

"Yes." Logan took it from her and turned it back, scribbled side up. "See here, when the detective sneaks out of the basement through the door leading to the root cellar…"

"Where did the root cellar come from?" Leigh frowned.

"Chapter one—you didn't read it."

"Oh. Okay."

"Can we continue now? Me doing the

writing—you typing?" Logan asked with amusement.

"Sure."

His cell rang in his pocket and he stood, checking the caller ID. His expression darkened.

"If you have to answer that, go ahead. I think I can make out the rest…if I squint really hard." But the light moment between them had disappeared.

"I'm sorry, it's important," he said as it rang again. Moving away, he answered the call.

Leigh watched his long, anxious strides as he paced the backyard. In the silence of the neighborhood, it was impossible not to hear his side of the conversation, despite the distance he put between them.

She felt a pang of guilt listening, but she couldn't help it. She was curious about him. Really curious. Since their first night working together, she'd tried to resist the urge to look him up on the computer, but that afternoon she'd caved. Not that she'd learned anything about his personal life.

"Yes, of course I have time to speak to

her.… Hi, sweetheart, you're up late," he said, glancing at his watch.

Sweetheart?

"How was school today?" she heard him ask.

It sounded as though he was talking to a child. His?

"Give them time, they'll come around. You're the coolest kid I know."

The concern in his voice touched her.

"That's great. I can't wait to see it.… I know, I miss you, too…just another couple of weeks.…"

Couple of weeks for what? Man, she had to stop eavesdropping. His call was none of her business.

"Okay, be good for your mom.… I love you." He disconnected the call and Leigh watched as he stood there for a second longer. He turned back toward her and their eyes met momentarily, before she quickly returned hers to the laptop screen.

Logan climbed the few steps to the gazebo and sat back on the bench. "Sorry about that."

"No problem." *Don't ask questions.* It was none of her business.

"Where did we leave off?"

"The detective is going downstairs," Leigh said. Clearly, he wasn't about to explain the call.

"Right." Logan cleared his throat, then stood again. "That was my daughter."

She fought to conceal her surprise. Never would she have pegged him for a father. How old was the girl? Did that mean he was married? Divorced? Where was she? Despite the insane curiosity mounting within her, she struggled to respect his privacy. "Really, Logan, that's your business."

Quietly, he rejoined her on the bench. "Okay, sorry, tell me again—where were we?"

"The detective's going downstairs…." Leigh prodded, studying him. The little piece of himself he'd displayed in those few seconds had revealed a different side of the man she was getting to know.

A man she wanted to get to know even better.

CHAPTER THREE

"OKAY, GUYS, CLIMB IN." Leigh opened the sliding side door of her minivan and hid a yawn as she helped the kids in. She couldn't remember the last time she'd been up so late on a weeknight. The progress was slow because of her inexpert typing and Logan's inability to decipher his own writing, but he'd been happy with the work they'd been able to accomplish in five hours.

Despite her previous claim that scary books didn't interest her, the more she read, the more engaged she was becoming. Enough so that she'd struggled with apprehension returning to her dark house alone just before midnight.

Unable to sleep, she'd stayed awake reading the first half of the first book in the series.

"Move all the way to the back, guys," Leigh told the Myer twins as she got in to do up their seat belts. David and Joshua Myers, eight, had a PD day from school, and she'd volunteered to babysit for their mom. Melody Myers worked three jobs since the death of her husband several years before and rarely asked for help.

"Where are we going Miss Leigh?" four-year-old Isabel Miller asked.

Leigh only winked as she climbed through the seats and jumped down from the van.

They all stared at her, hopeful.

"It's a surprise," she said as she closed the sliding door.

"Where *are* you taking them?" The deep voice of the man behind her made her jump.

Her hand flew to her chest as she turned. "Logan, you startled me."

"I'll try to stop doing that."

"I'd appreciate that."

"I saw your lights on last night. Thought you said the book wouldn't get to you." He shoved his hands in his pockets and rocked back on his heels.

"Yeah, well, I hadn't expected you to be such a good writer." Her gaze met his. He was actually a very attractive man, especially when his features softened and he didn't appear irritated at the world. His dark, wavy hair needed a trim and his week-old beard was scruffy, but she suspected he cleaned up quite nicely.

"I'll accept that backhanded compliment," he said, nodding toward the van. "Road trip?"

Leigh yawned. "Yes, if I can keep my eyes open. I haven't been up that late in a while." She lowered her voice and leaned in to say, "I'm taking the kids to the corn maze." A faint musky cologne reached her nose. He smelled good.

"Corn maze?" His brow furrowed. "What's that?"

"Shhhh...." She looked over her shoulder to make sure the kids hadn't heard. "You're kidding, right?" He'd never heard of a corn maze? When she was a child, the corn maze had been one of her favorite outings during harvest, whenever they were lucky enough to be in Brookhollow.

"No."

“You really are a city boy, aren’t you?”

“Hardly ever venture past the skyscrapers. So, are you going to enlighten me or am I going to have to look it up for myself?”

“It’s a maze made of out cornstalks at the Monroe family farm.” She paused, wondering if she should invite him along. How would the kids’ parents react? He was still a stranger after all. After several nights working with him, she still didn’t know him very well. She still couldn’t believe he was a father.

Logan cleared his throat. “I can’t go,” he said, staring at the sidewalk.

Had she asked him? “Did I invite you?”

“No, but you were struggling with whether to or not.”

Her mouth opened.

“Part of my job as a writer is to observe human behavior,” he explained. “I could read your expression.”

“Oh. Well, you’re welcome to come along if you want,” she said, glancing at her watch. “But we should get going.” She walked around to the driver’s side and opened the door.

"I really can't. I'm doing a school visit at Brookhollow High this morning."

He was what?

"Don't look so surprised."

"Sorry, I just, um, you *do* surprise me, that's all."

"Good. So, gazebo at six?"

"Of course," Leigh said as she closed the door. Feeling unexpectedly disappointed that he wasn't going with them, she pulled the van away from the curb and turned onto Cedar Street, all of a sudden looking forward to six o'clock.

LOGAN SLID INTO a corner booth at Joey's Diner on Main Street ten minutes later, wearing a satisfied smile. The fifties-style, family-owned-and-operated restaurant hadn't changed one bit. A group of older men sat on red-and-white-striped bar stools at the counter drinking coffee and reading newspapers, and the booth in the corner was occupied by a group of women playing bridge. A young waitress leaned on her elbows on the counter chatting with an older woman, whom he recognized. He couldn't remember her name, but he was great with faces. He searched her apron for a name tag as she wrapped cutlery in paper napkins. Tina. That's right. She and her husband, Joey Miller, owned the place. Noticing him, she nodded at the young woman.

The girl, April by her name tag, stood and smiled as she approached. "Hi there. Coffee?" She held the steaming pot and turned over the white ceramic coffee cup on the table.

"Yes, please. Could I also get a menu?" The smell of bacon coming from the kitchen was making his mouth water. He wasn't sure exactly what else he wanted, but definitely bacon.

"This must be your first time at Joey's," April said.

"No, but it's been a while."

She lifted his coffee cup and, picking up the paper place mat, full of advertisements, she turned it over. "There you go. We serve breakfast until eleven," she said, pointing to the eclectic selection. "I'll give you a few minutes to decide?"

"Yes, thank you." Logan scanned the list. What he really wanted was more of those muffins from Ginger Snaps, but by the sign on the front door they weren't open for business yet.

"So, where is Jonathan taking you for your anniversary tonight?" he heard Tina ask as she refilled ketchup bottles in a booth a few feet away.

April sighed. "The Haunted Hike at Monroe's." She rolled her eyes as she collected the empty salt and pepper shakers from the nearby tables.

"For your anniversary? That's hardly romantic.... I thought you said tonight might be the night."

The young woman shot a glance toward the men at the counter and placed her fingers to her lips. Nobody looked up. Logan quickly went back to perusing the menu. "Shh...maybe I was wrong. I'm starting to think he's never going to ask. I mean, we've been together four years now...."

Logan set the menu aside. Bacon and eggs it was. He took a sip of his coffee.

"Ready to order?" his lovelorn waitress asked, coming back.

He pointed to the chalkboard menu

near the door. "I'll have your special—the bacon and eggs, hash browns and toast."

She scribbled on her order pad. "White, whole wheat or multigrain?"

"White is fine, thanks," he answered, quickly adding as she turned to go, "Um, I didn't mean to eavesdrop, but what was it you mentioned about a haunted hike?"

Moving his coffee cup, she turned his place mat over yet again. She pointed to the small ad in the corner. "Monroe's Haunted Hike tour. It's at the family's farm, just outside town—where the pumpkin patch is…and the Christmas-tree farm…. You have no idea where I'm talking about, do you?" she said, tucking her pen behind her ear.

"I'm not from around here."

"Oh. Well, then where…?"

"California."

In truth, he wasn't actually from anywhere in particular. His birth certificate said he was born in Oakland, but since then he'd moved from one foster home to another in every city from Los Angeles to Fresno, until running away at fifteen and hitching rides out East.

"Are you here visiting family...or friends?" April asked.

The only family he had was Amelia and she was half a world away. His few friends were all back in the city. Moving around so much as a kid made developing lifelong friendships nearly impossible and besides most people only used you or let you down. "Nope. Just here to get some peace and quiet," he offered when she remained silent.

She glanced at his hand. "Trying to take it easy while your hand heals?"

"Actually I broke my wrist here...in my quest for peace and quiet."

"How did you manage to do that?" she asked, sitting on the bench on the other side of the booth.

Logan stared at her. *By all means, sit down, why don't you?* In New York, it was understood that everybody was on a tight timeline. And that your business was your own. "I was...hanging a sign."

Recognition crossed the woman's face. "Aw, good for Leigh, she's been talking about getting that sign put up for quite a while."

He did a double take. “You know which sign I…?” Shaking his head, he added, “Well, it didn’t get hung.” He held up the cast.

“Let me guess, she was trying to use that rickety old ladder?” She turned. “Mom, how many times have we told Leigh to get rid of that ladder?”

Tina, behind the counter, waved a hand. “Too many.”

“Anyway, I hope her luck starts to change.”

“What do you mean? What’s wrong with her luck?” Might help explain why he’d found her hiding from the ex-husband’s new wife the other day.

April’s eyes widened and she scrambled out of the booth. “Oh, nothing, I’m just babbling. Anyway, the Monroe Farm is hard to miss, just go down Main Street—”

Logan held up his good hand. “Whoa, go back. What did you mean?”

She bit her lip and shifted from one foot to another under Logan’s insistent gaze. She sat back in the booth. “I really shouldn’t be talking about this.”

"That's right, you shouldn't," her mother said, wiping a table nearby.

"I just meant that Leigh has had a rough few years…with her divorce." April turned to her mother. "Mom, do you want to jump in here?"

Tina paused near the table and grabbed April's order pad. "Nope, I'm not having Leigh angry at me. I'll go place your order." She clucked her tongue as she sauntered off to the kitchen.

The waitress toyed with the edge of the napkin. "You know, Mom's right."

Logan took the napkin from her and let the girl off the hook. "You know what, don't say any more. If I want to know about Leigh, I'll ask her."

The night before, Leigh hadn't questioned him about Amelia even though he suspected she'd been dying to know more. He needed to respect her privacy the way she'd respected his.

The door of the café chimed as a couple entered and waved to the men at the counter. "Be right with you guys," April said, then turned back to Logan. "Monroe's is straight down Main Street, and just as you pass the city limit sign heading onto the highway, you take the exit toward Pocomoke River. The farm is just a few miles south." She paused. "You won't be able to walk there, it's too far, and I'm guessing driving must be tough with that cast. If you want, you can go with my boyfriend!"

He laughed. "I'll keep that in mind. Thanks." He couldn't help but feel for the woman's boyfriend, even though she was joking. Kendra had called him the world's most unromantic and clueless man she'd ever known. It amazed him that their relationship had lasted as long as it did. "Have you been?" he asked.

"Yeah…our first date, actually. He thought it was a good idea then, too." She scoffed. "I clung to him the entire time." Her face softened a little at the memory.

"Could be why he's taking you there tonight."

She smiled. "Could be you're right."

Ha, maybe he did get romance sometimes.

THE ORANGE PUMPKIN patch sign at the entrance of the Monroe Farm was barely visible and the children in the back of the van had already started squealing.

"I knew it," Dylan said proudly, raising himself higher in his booster seat to get a better view as Leigh turned slowly onto the long drive leading onto the family farm.

"Are we going to get pumpkins?" Melissa asked.

"Can we have hot chocolate?" Michael asked.

Leigh smiled at them in the rearview mirror. "Yes and yes," she said, parking the van in the large open field where a few other vehicles and two school buses were parked. People from all over the region visited every fall for their pumpkins and later in the year for their Christmas trees. Shutting off the engine, she unlocked her seat belt and turned to face the eager expressions. "First, rules—let's hear 'em."

"Everyone stays together."

"Find a friend and hold hands."

"No straying from designated areas."

"No running or climbing on anything but the hay bales."

Leigh nodded at the chorus of replies.

"Great, and last one for this outing—only pick a pumpkin you can carry back to the van yourself because I won't be able to carry more than one myself. Everyone got it?"

A series of eager nods responded.

"Good, hats and gloves on." She scanned the row of kids. "Okay, let's go."

The Myers twins. She hadn't considered how they might feel being here. Brad, the youngest and only boy in the Monroe family, had been driving the car their dad was in when he died. While their father's former best friend and bandmate had left Brookhollow for good the day of the funeral, she wasn't clear how the Myers felt about the Monroes. All she knew was that Patrick Myers' parents refused to speak to the family after losing their only son.

She was relieved to see that the boys had partnered up with the two smallest children in the group to head toward the trail. Clearly, they weren't bothered by this surprise trip. Kids were resilient that way. It never ceased to amaze Leigh how life persevered in the face of such tragedy.

She swallowed a lump in her throat.

Ultimately, the boys would be affected by being raised by a solitary parent, wouldn't they? The absence of a father had to have some effect?

The baby she would adopt would be faced with a similar upbringing.... "Are you coming, Miss Leigh?" Josh Myers asked.

"Yes." She forced a smile, pushing the unsettling thought from her mind. These boys were two of the sweetest, mild-mannered, obedient boys she had the pleasure of minding. Clearly, their single-parent home wasn't having any ill effects on their personalities. "Let's go."

GROWING UP IN countless foster homes and later living on the street had prepared Logan for anything life could throw at him, or so he thought. Now, standing in front of a classroom of seventeen-year-olds, he wasn't so sure. He wasn't sure what unnerved him more, the few eager kids in the front row perched on the edge of their desk chair, a blank piece of paper in front of them, pen clasped tightly in hand, or the uninterested cool kids in the back row who were clearly taking the class for extra credit. Disappointing the first and boring the second was another source of tension to add to his overgrowing pile.

"Everyone, this is Logan Walters, a *New York Times* bestselling author of the..." Standing next to him at the front of the creative-writing class, Principal Carter turned to him. "Sorry, I can't remember the name of your series."

"The Van Gardener Series!" a kid in the front row supplied.

"That's right," Logan said with a nod to the boy. At least one of the students had read his work. Though he wasn't sure if that was entirely a good thing or not. If they followed the series, they also knew about the six-year gap between books four and five. He wasn't sure what kind of credibility that gave him as a writer.

"Well, you have one fan in the room already," Randi said, tapping his shoulder as she moved past him. "I'll leave it up to you, then." She made her way to the back of the classroom and took an empty seat, motioning for the boy sitting next to her to remove his feet from the desk.

"Hi, everyone." Logan cleared his throat

as he moved closer to the desk in front of the high-school students. In his room that morning he'd considered calling in sick, but word would've gotten back to the bed-and-breakfast owners and he'd have felt compelled to fake it the rest of the day.

What was he doing here?

When he looked out at these kids, all he could think about was his daughter and how much he missed her. He shouldn't be here. He should be writing. He should be back in New York presenting his lawyer with some more brilliant reasons why Amelia needed him.

He was beginning to suspect that maybe she didn't need him. Maybe nobody did....

The kid who read his books looked back over his shoulder at the teacher, who was staring at Logan, clearly concerned.

He searched his brain for something to say, convinced he was wasting their time as much as his. "For those of you taking this class because you actually enjoy writing, what do you enjoy about it?"

He used to know his answer to that, but over the years with deadlines and promotion and public events, he wasn't sure anymore. He couldn't remember the last time he sat down to write because he had the urge to create something.

When he'd written book five after the long dry spell, it had come from a place of desperation, of not knowing what else to do. As it had when he was a teenager, writing had once again saved him from despair as he'd poured his emotions into that penultimate installment in the series.

But this final book was just a burden.

A young girl in the second row raised a hand.

"Yes…your name?"

"Kelly."

"Okay, Kelly. What do you love about writing?" he asked, leaning on the edge of the teacher's desk.

"I love that I get to live different lives through my characters. Small-town life is okay, I guess, but through my stories I get to explore other possibilities," she said.

Good answer, and one his teenage self could have related to. "What kind of characters do you normally write?"

Her cheeks flushed and she lowered her

eyes as her classmates started to laugh. "Superheroes."

"Awesome," Logan said, silencing the kids who were clearly used to giving this girl grief. He could relate to her uphill battle to be taken seriously. He'd been there himself. "Superheroes are very popular in today's market. If you can create something unique, exciting, something we haven't seen before, you could do real well with that. Anyone else care to comment on why they write?"

A young man with short, gelled hair in the middle row nearest the window spoke up. "I'm Kent. I like writing because it's freeing."

He nodded. Freeing. At one time he would have agreed, but he hadn't thought about writing that way for a very long time. "What do you do when you find that you can't write?"

"You mean like writer's block?" A girl with red curls hanging past her shoulders asked.

"Yeah." He could feel the teacher studying him intently and it took all his strength not to look her way. No doubt she was wondering why Principal Carter had asked him to come today.

"I go for a walk, get away from it for a while."

"I pick up another project."

The suggestions rang out, all good, but nothing he hadn't already tried.

"Maybe you're going in the wrong direction," a guy said from the back of the room.

Logan perked up, pointing to the kid in the far corner. In his New York Giants football jersey and torn jeans, Logan would have pegged him as part of the extra-credit crowd. "What do you write?"

The boy scoffed. "I don't write. I play football," he said, a little too quickly.

Meaning he didn't want anyone to know he wrote.

"Okay, well, can you explain what you mean for the benefit of those of us who do write?"

"Not that I know anything about it… but if characters dictate where the plot goes—"

"Happens all the time, yes," Logan agreed.

"Then maybe writer's block is trying to force the characters in a direction they don't want to go."

Smart kid. Logan ran his good hand through his hair. "So, what do you suggest if, say, a writer was to come up against a block like this… Sorry, what's your name?"

"Brody."

"What should I…I mean anyone suffering from writer's block do when their characters resist them?"

All eyes turned on the boy, and in that moment his demeanor visibly changed to complete disinterest. "I don't know, man. I told you, I'm not a writer."

"Of course not." Damn, so close. Maybe he should hire this kid to help him with his book after school. He could probably type, too. "Thanks, Brody."

"Whatever," the boy mumbled.

"LEIGH…" ANGELA CONWAY STRUGGLED to catch her breath as she caught up to the group in the parking lot of the pumpkin patch.

Leigh cringed before slowly turning to face the woman. “Hi, Angela.”

“I’ve been chasing you…for about ten… minutes,” she said, placing her hands around her six-month bulge in the front of her fall coat.

Across the parking lot, Leigh could see Neil Conway fastening the seat belt of their two-year-old, Mason, in the back of their SUV. He glanced their way and offered a shrug and what-can-you-do smile before climbing inside the driver side.

“Sorry, I didn’t notice,” Leigh mumbled, opening the side door to the van. “Kids, lay your pumpkins on the ground and climb in. I’ll put them all in the back.”

“What if you get them mixed up?” Isabel asked.

“I’m sure you guys will know your own pumpkins,” she said, helping the little girl into her booster seat.

“So, Leigh, you never did get back to me regarding space in the New Year,” Angela said.

“Well, I never actually know until a month before and, honestly, the day care is running at full capacity right now." It wasn't a lie.

"But Ashley said she was hoping to stay on full-time."

"Yeah, that's not definite yet." The idea of minding her ex-husband's kids was tough to swallow. Mason and Jonas were adorable, but they represented everything she hadn't been able to give Neil. They would be a constant reminder that the inability to have the family they'd wanted had been all her fault.

"Oh. Well, once you know..." Angela's disappointment was too much. After all, it wasn't her fault that things hadn't worked out for Leigh and Neil.

"You will be the first to know." Leigh regretted the words as soon as they escaped her lips. She'd never rush to let Angela know about available space.

"Thanks, Leigh." She turned to leave, then paused. "You're just so wonderful with them, you know?" She looked as though she wanted to say more, but shook her head. "Anyway, let me know."

Leigh watched the woman waddle across the gravel lot to where Neil waited. Mom, dad, two and a half kids—the American family. Everything she'd wanted for herself.

"You okay, Miss Leigh?" David asked, picking up several pumpkins and carrying them to the back of the van.

"Yes, I'm fine," she said, picking up two more and struggling to open the back door to put them inside.

"You're going to say yes eventually, you know," the eight-year-old shocked her by saying. Clearly gossip about her divorce and Neil's second marriage circulated the Myers home.

"Why do you say that?" she asked, setting the remaining pumpkins inside and shutting the door.

"Because you love kids."

CHAPTER FOUR

LEAVING THE HIGH SCHOOL, Logan continued down Main Street. The silence was almost unnerving that time of day. No one was around except several workers replacing a streetlight bulb a few feet away. A rickety pickup truck drove past at a leisurely pace, and the old driver inside waved. Logan nodded. Brookhollow was the kind of place he would love to have lived in as a child. A place where neighbors looked out for one another. No one had ever looked out for him. He'd learned early that trusting people would only lead to heartache.

Then he'd let his guard down with Kendra, and she'd only proven that his distrust had been bang on.

To his right, he noticed Dog Eared Books. Bright yellow sale signs were pasted to the inside of the store windows, and several tables out front displayed fifty-cent secondhand books. He couldn't help wondering how many of these sale tables his books had found their way to over the years.

Crossing the street, he scanned the tables before going inside. Nope, none of his.

As he was looking through the storefront, a rolltop desk caught his attention immediately and he opened the door to go inside. Except he couldn't get past a stack of boxes in the entrance to reach the desk.

He peered around the side to see a middle-aged woman on a ladder toward the back of the shop. Great, another ladder. For the rest of this trip, his feet would remain on the ground.

"Hello," he called out.

The woman turned. "Oh, hi. Come on in," she said, climbing down from the ladder, several books in her arms. She tossed them into an open box on the floor labeled Donate.

"I would but I can't get around these boxes."

"Sorry.... Here, let me move these." She reached for the top box, setting it aside.

"I'd help, but..." He held up his cast.

"No problem. I've been moving boxes around all day," she mumbled, shoving the last box aside to give him room.

The two-story space was a book lover's dream with its floor-to-ceiling shelves and a spiraling staircase leading to the second floor and antique furniture was scattered throughout. "Is that a Cutler?"

Pushing her hair back from her face, the woman followed to where he was looking at the desk. "From the early nineteenth century," she confirmed. "Like it?"

"Like it? Are you kidding? The closest one to this condition I found was an 1878 replica in Great Britain, but I'd have to donate a kidney to afford the shipping cost."

Maybe his appreciation for the artisan workmanship of this beautiful antique came from his lack of connection to family—he had no idea. Maybe his need to own one of these beauties derived from the fact that they were usually family heirlooms, handed down generation to generation, rarely leaving a single family's hands. That kind of...heritage and family story line...was something he could only read about. Or write about. But since receiving his first advance check ten years before, he'd been looking for a Cutler rolltop oak writing desk.

He ran his good hand along the extended brass escutcheon, admiring the authenticating Cutler embossing.

"Well, unfortunately this one would cost even more. It's a family heirloom brought over from Great Britain in the late 1800s by my very great ancestors."

Of course it was, he thought, stepping back from it.

"It's survived moves across the country, being stored in attics and basements for decades, only to make its way here with my great-grandmother almost a hundred years ago." She polished the oak-stained wood finish where he'd left his fingerprints, then turned to study him.

"Danielle O'Connor," she said. "Was there something in particular you were hoping to find today? A lot of things are packed away, but believe it or not, it's an organized mess, so I might be able to find it."

"Logan Walters."

She did a double take. “Logan—”

“Walters,” he finished for her. “Just… saw the desk. That’s all.”

“Well, Mr. W-Walters,” she began to stutter, “feel free to browse. Just be careful of all the boxes.”

He scanned a selection of new releases along the far wall. “When’s the store closing?” he asked.

“December thirty-first. I don’t see the point in staying open into the new year.”

“Not enough business?”

Danielle gave a small laugh. “We didn’t have enough business when we first opened this store eighty-eight years ago. Now keeping the store open is costing too much,” she said sadly.

“Eighty-eight years?” A landmark in the community.

“Yes. My great-grandmother opened it with the money she made off the sale of the one and only book she ever wanted to write.”

“What was it called?”

“*The Way Home.* It was a wonderful story about a woman’s—”

"Struggle for equality in the late 1950s, I've read it."

She looked at him in disbelief. "*You* read a feminist title written by a lesser-known author?"

"In university I took a women's literature course. Required reading, but a great story."

"Wow, Great-grandma would be impressed."

"So, if the store's been open that long, this building must be rather old." He could tell upgrades had been made to the space, as the wood finishing on the floor was darker in certain spots on the original hardwood floor—obviously certain planks had been replaced, and the moldings along the base of the shop walls were new, though they were designed to look like the original handcrafted decorative adornments bordering the walls.

"A hundred and forty-three years old. It used to be a law office. That's where the rest of this older furniture came from. When it closed, they left everything behind."

"So this is a heritage landmark building."

She nodded.

"Have you looked into the funding available for businesses operating in buildings like this?"

"Yes. Unfortunately we didn't qualify."

"What about a preservation grant? This store has been a part of Brookhollow for so long, certainly it would qualify for some help." So much had already changed in the small town, it would be a shame to lose another small business. He scanned the shop. "Do you have a computer in here?"

"Over here," Danielle said, leading the way to the cash-register desk. She opened a laptop and punched in her password, then opening the internet, she slid it toward him.

With his left hand, Logan did a search for the type of grant he suspected she could apply for and after several seconds the website for the New Jersey Heritage Committee lit up the screen. "See?" he said as he slid the laptop toward her.

Danielle scanned the page. "If I could qualify for one of these, I could keep the store open, at least until I retire. Heaven knows my kids wouldn't be interested in running the place. Thank you, Mr. Walters. I'm grateful for your help."

"Grateful enough to sell me that desk?" He nodded toward the Cutler. If she said yes, he'd carry it back to the B & B himself, busted hand and all.

She laughed. "Almost, but not quite."

Logan shrugged. "Had to try."

LEIGH OPENED HER dresser drawer and scanned the mess. No, nothing new had found its way into it since the last time she'd torn it apart, looking for something to wear. She blew her hair off her forehead. She was being ridiculous. It didn't matter what she wore.

She caught a glimpse of her reflection in the mirror. She'd set her curls and stained her lips. Her reflection taunted her.

The truth was she'd been looking forward to seeing Logan all day and wanted to look nice. Even if all he saw when he looked at her was ten capable typing fingers. Debatably capable.

Groaning, she reached into the drawer

for her black V-neck sweater as the doorbell rang.

She tugged it over her head as she made her way down the hall, careful not to crush her curls. She pulled her hair free from beneath the fabric, smoothing down the static, and opened the door. "Logan? I thought we were meeting at the gazebo?"

He shivered in a gust of wind that blew a trail of leaves across her front porch. His eyes narrowed. "Did you do something different with your face?"

Leigh rubbed her lips together, trying to conceal the stain. "No…it's just some makeup," she said, wiping them.

"Oh, did you have plans tonight?"

Leigh cleared her throat. "No, I've just had it on all day…must have forgotten to wash it off," she lied through a deep breath.

Logan moved closer. "Your hair is different, too."

So much for him not noticing. "I curl it sometimes." She wrapped her arms around her midsection and rubbed her sides for warmth. The fog was rolling in on the breeze, and the air was damp and chilled. "So, are we not working tonight?"

"Well, we made a lot of progress last night. And I've, uh, I've run out of new content." He shoved his hands in his pockets and rocked back and forth on his heels.

"Right." Leigh frowned. "So, what's the problem? You dictate…slowly, of course… and I'll type."

"It's not that easy." Logan ran his left hand through his hair and studied his hiking boots.

"To create on the spot?" Leigh waved a hand and reached for a coat on the hook beside the door. "Give me a second and I'll—"

"No, Leigh, you don't understand. I got nothing. I don't know what else to write. For the first time in my career, I've hit a wall and honestly don't know a way around it," he said, pacing the creaky wooden planks. "I've had writer's block before and it was just a matter of pushing through, writing all the wrong words until the right words come. But this…this is something else entirely. There are no words." He paced faster.

Leigh was unsure what to say. "Maybe… maybe if you just took a break and got away from it this evening? Did something completely different? You might be able to see your story fresh when you get back to it tomorrow. I don't know…."

Logan cleared his throat and reached into his jeans pocket. "That reminds me." He pulled out a tiny, crinkled piece of paper and handed it to her.

Taking it, she frowned. "A piece of Joey's menu?"

He motioned. "Turn it over."

The Haunted Hike ad from the Monroe Farm. "Well, if it's scary inspiration you need, you're sure to find it there." She handed him back the ad.

He shrugged. "I guess it couldn't hurt. As it is, I've got nothing." He studied her for a moment. "So I guess that means you're off the hook tonight. I'll let you know if and when I need you…. I mean your typing services." He turned and bounded down the steps two at a time.

"I'll go with you," she called, sliding her arms into her coat and grabbing her house keys.

Logan turned on the path. "I didn't ask..."

Leigh closed and locked her door and joined him on the pathway. She wrapped her pale pink scarf around her neck. "I know, but you wanted to." She cocked her head to the side. "I can read people, too."

THE HEADLIGHTS OF Leigh's minivan cut through the deep fog as she turned onto the gravel driveway to the Monroe Farm for the second time that day. Two volunteers, wearing orange flag vests, motioned the way to the field where dozens of other vehicles were parked.

Logan peered through the windshield. "I don't see anything decorated." He'd been expecting to see lights or signs, any indication of a Halloween event taking place, but the parking lot was dark, lit only by the streetlamps on the side of the road and the occasional headlights of other cars. Spooky atmosphere in itself.

"A shuttle bus will pick us up near the farmhouse to bring us to the hike's starting point." She glanced at the time on the dash. "If we hurry, we can make the first one at seven," she said, grabbing her toque from the backseat and tugging it on. "Ready?" she asked as she cut the engine and reached for her matching pink mittens.

It didn't escape his notice that she didn't flinch at covering what had obviously been an effort with her hair. His ex would rather freeze in the cold than ruin her hair or makeup. "Yeah, I'm ready. Let's go."

Opening the passenger door, he hopped down, zipping his thermal jacket higher. He shivered in the damp, bone-chilling air and met Leigh in front of the minivan. The thick fog drifting over the grass made it difficult to see farther than a few feet, so he stayed close to her. The faint smell of jasmine perfume he'd first noticed in the van reached his nose and he smiled. She had gone to some trouble getting ready that evening. He wasn't hating that idea.

"This way," Leigh said.

Another orange-vested volunteer smiled in greeting as they approached the gate. "Hey, Leigh. Weren't you here earlier today with the kids?" The young boy held a stack of glow sticks in one hand and a flashlight in the other.

"Yes, I'm back. This time for the haunted hike." She gestured to Logan. "This is Logan Walters. He's staying at the bed-and-breakfast—" Realizing what she'd said, she quickly looked at him to make sure she hadn't given away too much of his personal information. But Logan just smiled. "Uh, this is Jack Monroe. His family owns the farm."

Logan extended a hand. "Nice to meet you."

"You, too." Jack glanced between the two of them curiously. "You'd better hurry, the next shuttle leaves in a few minutes. Doug's leading the seven o'clock tour." He cracked two glow sticks for them. "For additional light. The trail can get quite dark in areas. Just head to the booth along the back of the house for your tickets," he said, pointing the way down the dimly lit gravel path.

"Thanks, Jack." Leigh waved.

Logan fastened the string on his glow stick and wrapped it around his neck.

"Clever," Leigh said with a smile.

"Here," Logan said, taking hers and knotting the string. Stopping in front of her, he placed it over her head, then gently lifted her hair above the string, allowing his hand to linger on the softness a second too long. Leigh's gaze met his. "There you go," he said, quickly moving away.

"Thanks," she said as they continued toward the ticket booth in silence.

A young girl greeted them behind the ticket counter. "Hi, Leigh. You made it just in time." She picked up a walkie-talkie from the counter. "Doug, we have two more riders. Over."

"Okay, we'll wait. Tell them to hurry. Over."

"Six dollars each, please." She rubbed her bare hands together for heat.

"I got it." Logan reached into his back pocket and retrieved his wallet.

Leigh reached into her pocket. "No, that's okay," she said, shaking her head and unfolding a ten-dollar bill.

"No, really, Leigh." Logan lowered his voice. "It's the least I can do for your help." He suspected the residents in the small town were curious about who he was and why he was spending time with the child-care provider. From her availability in helping him that week, he didn't think she was involved with anyone…he never saw anyone visiting during the day. He placed his hand over hers, pushing her money aside as he handed over a twenty-dollar bill. "Keep the change." The money was being donated to the local food bank.

"Thank you. Here are your tickets. Just head around back and have fun," she said in a spooky tone.

Logan shoved his wallet back in his pocket.

Leigh stared at the loose gravel under her feet as he fell into step beside her. "You didn't have to do that."

"It was nothing, really. I do plan to compensate you for the time you're giving up, helping me. I'm not sure I mentioned that."

Leigh gestured to his cast. "That's not necessary. You wouldn't even need my help if you hadn't broken your wrist trying to help me."

Logan frowned. "I wish I could blame my lack of progress on this injury." After the last letter from Dillon and McKay Family Law, stating that Kendra wanted to move to California with Amelia, all forward momentum had ground to a halt. The idea that he might be faced with the choice of only seeing Amelia twice a year or moving to California was all he could think about.

Maybe Brody was right, maybe he *was* forcing the plot in a direction the characters didn't want to go.

"Let's hope this helps," Leigh said as she climbed onto the shuttle bus. "Hi, Doug." She handed the driver her ticket.

"Aha, I knew we'd finally get you out here," he said with a wink.

"Yeah, well, this may be my first and last. This is Logan Walters, he's a guest at the B-and-B."

Logan handed Doug his ticket. "Nice to meet you."

Doug's eyes widened and a broad smile spread across his face. He moved his hat farther onto his forehead and squinted in the dim lighting of the bus as he studied Logan. "You're not *the* Logan Walters, are you? Author of the Van Gardener series?"

So a few people in town had heard of him and his books. "Afraid so." Logan nodded and extended a hand.

"Great to meet you. I've read the first four books in the series. I heard the last two are on the way." He looked hopeful.

"So I've been told." Out of the corner of his eye he noticed Leigh staring. He was grateful she didn't reveal to his fan the trouble he was having finishing the final installment.

"Well, grab a seat. It's an honor to have you along for the tour." Doug closed the shuttle door.

Logan followed Leigh to the remaining empty seats near the back of the shuttle bus, aware of the scrutinizing, curious stares as they passed. He sat on the aisle seat next to her. "Thanks for not calling me out as a fraud up there."

Leigh touched his bare hand. "You're not a fraud. I've seen your work, Logan. It's really good."

Logan stared at the point of contact, the heat from Leigh's delicate, tiny hand burning into his flesh. The comforting warmth enveloping him was foreign—Kendra's touch had been far from comforting. During his childhood, moving from one house to another, physical closeness and warmth had been rare. Even the nicer families had been kind, but cool toward their foster kids. Getting too attached made it painful on everyone when the children were reassigned to new families.

He would have thought that the lack of permanency in his childhood would prepare him for Kendra's leaving, but the opposite was true. For the first time, with Kendra and Amelia he'd felt as though he belonged somewhere, as though he was a part of a family. Now he was once again alone.

He turned his hand, grasping Leigh's as he brought it to his lips, where he placed a soft kiss. "Thank you," he said against her warm skin.

She blushed but didn't pull away as they both kept their eyes on their joined hands.

"Okay, everyone, stay together on the trail and follow me," Doug announced a second later as the shuttle came to an abrupt stop.

Logan dropped Leigh's hand. Their gazes held a second, before Leigh turned away and stood.

"That was a quick ride." Her voice was

hoarse as she tried to make light of the exchange that had occurred between them. He noticed the slight shake of her hand as she poked a stray curl under her toque and followed him off the bus.

Doug stood in front of the signs marking the beginning of the hike: Do Not Enter After Dark, No Trespassing and Enter at Your Own Risk. His face adopted a serious expression as he held his lantern to his chin. The reflection of his darkened features in the thick, smoky fog was eerie and Logan heard Leigh gulp. "Last chance to turn back before we enter the haunted woods of shadows," Doug said in an echoing, hollow voice.

Logan glanced at Leigh. "You're sure you're okay with this? You look kind of spooked already," he whispered with a grin. Clearly this was not a place she would go on her own. She was doing this for him. He wondered, when was the last time someone did something just for her? Too long, he decided.

Leigh scoffed. "Of course, I'm fine."

"Have you always lied this much?" Logan asked as they followed Doug down the path. Soon the neon-green fluorescent light from the row of glow sticks was the only light other than tiny orange-and-white holiday lights illuminating the ground on their side of the trail.

"No, you seem to bring out the worst in me."

Crispy leaves crunched beneath their feet, and the wind howled and whistled—taped sound effect, Logan decided, since it hadn't been quite that blustery when they parked. The fog that continued to roll in, however, was real—and making it difficult to see far in front of them. Logan zipped his coat higher and wiggled his bare fingers beneath the cast. He stepped on a broken tree branch lying on the path and it snapped under his weight, the unexpected sound in the silence causing his heart to stop.

Leigh jumped and moved closer to him, her face pale in the green glow coming from around her neck.

He apologized as the family behind them laughed. "This scary stuff is really not your thing, huh?"

"I can't believe it's anyone's *thing*. Why

on earth do people like scaring the crap out of themselves?" She shivered, scanning the darkness.

"I guess it's the same reason people read my books. They want to feel as though things can work out. They want to feel scared, while all the while knowing things will be okay."

"Will things be okay? In your series, I mean?" She grew serious as she asked, her fear seemingly forgotten.

"Why do you ask?"

"Well, correct me if I'm wrong..." She paused, moving even closer and lowering her voice. "But it seems to me that the plot is heading in a certain direction...one that might be less than okay."

She could sense that already? His original plan to kill off Van Gardener in this last book was showing through in the writing? He frowned. That wasn't good. If he was going to risk an ending like this, it had to come from left field; fans couldn't be expecting it. "You know how I plan to end the book?"

"I could be wrong," she said quickly.

"You're not."

Doug paused near the first exhibit, a decrepit grave site. The headstones were weather-beaten and broken, and fresh bloody footprints came from the dug-up ground of the grave. "Here lies Dr. Ernstein…or at least he used to rest in peace here…looks like he may no longer be contained beneath six feet of heavy dirt." An eerie scream a few feet away in the woods caught the group's attention and everyone turned toward the sound.

A dark figure advanced toward them from the woods, wearing a stained, torn doctor's lab coat. Leigh moved to stand behind Logan as the ghoulish creature drew closer, arms outstretched, a grotesque, decaying face, eyes unseeing as he continued to wander the forest.

She let out a deep breath as it moved away. "Thank God," she said, but as she turned, a loud squeal escaped her. Another zombified creature peered directly over her shoulder. She clutched the back of Logan's coat with both hands and buried her face into the fabric, turning their bodies to put him between herself and the zombie. The young actor's eyes glinted with pride for having succeeded in terrifying her as he moved on to terrorize the rest of the group.

Logan turned slightly, taking her hands. "He's gone," he said with a laugh.

Leigh swiped his casted hand. "That wasn't funny."

"It was, actually," he said, composing himself. "You really didn't have to come along. You're terrified. And you know you're going to be targeted now—you're the perfect audience." He rubbed her arms and bent his knees to look into her wide eyes. Beautiful eyes. Kind eyes.

"I can handle it."

Logan didn't think twice before wrapping his arm around her waist as they continued on down the path of terror. "Are you sure? You, Leigh Norris, are a lot of things, but brave is not one of them."

CHAPTER FIVE

"IS THIS RIGHT, Miss Leigh?" Isabel asked, sitting on a chair in Leigh's kitchen behind the table where she cut the shape of a pumpkin out of orange construction paper early the next day.

Too early. Leigh hid a yawn as she nodded. "Yes, sweetie, that's great." She glued a set of googly eyes to a cutout of a ghost and handed it to Dylan. "Just set this on the window ledge to dry with the others and they should be ready for you to take home at the end of the day."

The oven timer chimed and Leigh grabbed her oven mitts from the counter. "Everyone stay in your seats, away from the oven, while I get the cookies," she said, before removing the tray of shortbread and placing them on the cooling rack above the stove.

"They smell yummy. Can we decorate them now?" Melissa asked, standing on her chair to peer at the shortbread cookies with interest.

"They have to cool first, and chairs are for bottoms." Leigh motioned for the little girl to sit as she removed her oven mitts and got out her decorating tools and bags of colored frosting and sprinkles.

The house phone rang and she scanned the messy kitchen for her cordless. She moved the art supplies and the baking dishes on the counter, guided by the muffled sound of the ringing. "Guys, have you seen the phone?" she asked, shuffling the loose sheets of construction paper on the table.

"Here it is," Isabel said, moving a bag of pipe cleaners. Instead of handing it over, she answered it. "Hello?"

Leigh put her hand on her hip and cocked her head to the side. She hid a grin as she waited.

The girl's eyebrows wove together as she listened. "Yeah, she's right here. Hold, please," she said, extending the phone to Leigh. "It's for you."

"You're kidding?" Chuckling, she took the phone. "Hello?" She cradled the phone against her shoulder as she got the milk out of the fridge. Then opening the dishwasher, she removed the clean plastic multicolored cups and placed them on the counter.

"Leigh Norris?" an unfamiliar voice asked.

"Yes, this is Leigh." Straightening, she turned and motioned for the noisy kids to quiet down. Very few people called her home phone anymore. She'd get rid of the landline altogether, but with operating the day care, it was safer in the case of an emergency.

"This is Michelle Bennett from the New Jersey Adoption Center."

Leigh's heart raced and her pulse thundered. Swallowing the lump in her throat and forcing her voice to remain steady, she said, "Hi, Ms. Bennett." The letter she'd received stating her deposit had arrived had indicated it would be months before she'd hear anything. That was only a little over two weeks ago. Was a call this soon a good thing or a bad thing?

"Have I caught you at a bad time?"

Leigh plugged her other ear to the shrill noises in the background and winced, moving out into the hallway. Letting the swinging door close halfway behind her, but keeping it propped open with her foot to keep an eye on the kids, she said, "No, not at all. I run a day care in my home," she explained. *Please don't let this woman form an opinion of my parenting skills based on the noise level in my home.*

"Oh, okay. Well, that explains the noise," Michelle said.

"Yes, I'm sorry. It's arts-and-crafts time. They can get…excitable." Leigh's hand shook and she switched the phone to the other ear.

"No apology necessary. Children having fun is a wonderful sound."

Leigh's shoulders relaxed. She liked Michelle Bennett already, she decided. "What can I do for you, Michelle?" Her nerves were jumping. Had she sent the wrong amount for the application? Had they found a reason to reject her application already?

"I was hoping to set up a time for an interview and home visit."

Leigh's mouth dropped and the phone slipped out of her hand. She blinked through a dizzy spell. "Already?" she managed to choke out when she'd grabbed the phone up again.

"Yes. I know it's probably sooner than you expected."

Leigh stammered, "Um…yes…."

"Well, if it's not a good time—"

"No, please excuse my hesitancy. I just hadn't expected to hear from anyone so soon, but this is wonderful," she said as she leaned against the wall in the hallway. Her knees felt like rubber and she didn't trust their ability to hold her upright. A home visit. Already. Excitement welled in her chest.

"Great. Would sometime next week work for you? I don't want to give you any false expectations, though. Be prepared for this process to take some time." The woman hesitated and then added, "But we do have a situation currently that we feel may be a fit."

Tears forced their way into her throat and she swallowed hard. “I understand.”

“So, next week? Monday?”

“Yes. I have the day-care children until five-thirty. Would six be okay?” Logan would have to do without her for an evening. If he was still here. The thought hit her with a wave of sadness.

If he knew what she was about to do, would he approve?

She heard Michelle hesitate. “If we need to meet earlier…” She’d figure something out. Maybe Ashley could work that afternoon and take the children to the playground on the corner.

“No, six will be fine. Most home visits are in the evening when couples are home from work. We’re flexible. I’ll see you then.”

“Great, thank you.” Leigh disconnected the call and held the phone to her chest. Her thoughts and emotions were indecipherable. A home visit…the first real step in the process. She could have a child sooner than she’d originally hoped or expected. Tears welled in her eyes and she swallowed the resurfacing lump in her throat as she leaned against the wall, her eyes fixed on the photo of her parents hanging on the wall across from her.

They didn't know of her plans yet. She hadn't wanted to tell too many people in case things didn't work out and yet, they were her parents. They loved her and she could only imagine that they would support her in this. Maybe they'd even come home more often when they became grandparents. The very idea took Leigh's breath away. She had to tell them. She would try to call them soon.

The swinging kitchen door opened and Melissa came out into the hall, her hand glued to a piece of construction paper. "Miss Leigh, I'm stuck."

Leigh bent to squeeze the little girl tight. She was so happy she thought her heart would explode. "Okay, let's go get you unstuck so we can decorate some cookies."

LEIGH GLANCED AT the call display on her cell phone as she answered on the third ring later that evening. Seconds before, the home phone had been ringing, but she hadn't found the cordless in time. "Hi, Rachel, sorry I'm late. I'm almost ready." She cradled the phone against her shoulder as she secured her hair behind her ear with a bobby pin.

"Don't rush, we're not going." Her cousin sounded upset.

"What? Why not?" Earlier that afternoon, when she'd called her to share her goods news about the home visit, Rachel had been excited about the Halloween party at the community hall that evening. Since the birth of the twins, Rachel and Nathan rarely went anywhere together without the children. They deserved a break, but finding someone to babysit five kids wasn't easy. And whenever there was an event in town, finding someone who wasn't attending was even harder.

"The Halloween costume doesn't fit," she said with a sigh. "Apparently I have more baby weight to lose than I'd thought." She sounded close to tears. "Losing the weight on the other three hadn't seemed this hard."

"I'm sure the costume can be made to fit, right?"

"No, it can't. I'm disgusting."

"No, you aren't. You're beautiful," Leigh heard Nathan say in the background.

She smiled. After thirteen years and five kids, the couple's relationship was as strong as it had always been. It was encouraging to see that things could work out.

"You have to say that. *You*'re the one who keeps making me fat," Rachel said to her husband, then into the phone, added, "Anyway, Leigh, I hope you hadn't canceled any plans for tonight. I think we'll just stay home."

Leigh scanned her closet. The witch's costume she wore every year for the day care children's Halloween party caught her eye. She was a little shorter than Rachel, but the dress was loose and flowy; it was sure to fit her cousin's motherly curves. "If you don't mind going as a witch, I have a costume you can wear," she said, taking it out and reaching for the black, pointed hat.

"Oh, were you planning to go to the party tonight? Oh, now I feel bad—"

"No, no, Rachel," Leigh interrupted. "It's just my day-care Halloween costume." She sat on the edge of her bed and tugged her flat leather boots over her skinny jeans.

"Are you sure?"

"I'll bring it right over."

"You're a lifesaver, Leigh."

Ten minutes later, Rachel inspected herself in the full-length mirror in the master suite of the family's quarters of the bed-and-breakfast.

Nathan whistled his approval, as he stared at his wife's fishnet stockings, showing quite a bit of her leg under the witch's dress.

Rachel looked at him. "I don't know..."

"Are you kidding me? You look amazing. You're wearing it." Nathan folded his arms. "Tell her, Leigh."

"You look great, Rachel."

"It's a little short." Rachel tugged it farther down her legs.

"You're a little taller than me. Trust me, I don't wear it that short around the kids," she was quick to explain.

Nathan gave her a pointed look.

"Oh, but for an adults party, it's perfect."

Rachel still didn't look convinced.

A horn honked outside.

Nathan stood and glanced through the curtain. "There's Luke and Vic. Are we going?" He paused hopefully.

Rachel hesitated a second longer, then said, "Fine...okay."

Nathan beamed.

"Great. Where are the kids?" Leigh stood and followed them out into the hall. She hadn't seen or heard them since she came in, which was odd.

"The babies are already asleep and the others are spending the night at Aunt Lindsay's." Rachel picked up her purse and led the way downstairs, baby monitor in hand.

"Really? Lindsay agreed to babysit?" Nathan's sister was a nurse at the local clinic and she was a fantastic aunt to the kids...but she didn't seem the type to be able to handle three kids for any period of time.

"Yes, she's dating a single dad from Beach Haven. He's in town with his daughter this week. She's trying to demonstrate her love of children." At the bottom of the stairs Rachel hesitated as Nathan gathered their coats from the front closet.

"Wow, easy night, then." She was a little disappointed, as she'd been looking forward to seeing the baby girls, but at least now she had time to talk to her parents. Leigh reached for the monitor, but Rachel clutched it tight, a worried expression crossing her face.

"Is everything okay?"

"Yes…no…. We just haven't been away from the twins before."

Leigh gave her a knowing smile. She saw parents' reluctance to leave their children all the time when they first started day care. "I understand. But they're already asleep. I'm sure they're out for the night."

"Come on, Rachel," Nathan pleaded.

Rachel slowly released the monitor. "Okay…you're right. The babies will be fine. They're in great hands. It's the older kids at Lindsay's I should be worried about." She forced a smile, but the worry remained in her eyes. Turning, she slid into the open coat Nathan held for her.

He untucked her hair from beneath the coat and handed her her mittens and scarf.

Rachel lingered at the open door.

"Rachel, they won't even know we're

gone," Nathan called, already at Luke's truck.

Victoria and Luke waved to Leigh.

Waving back, she gently nudged Rachel outside. She waved the monitor. "Don't worry, I got this."

Rachel released a nervous laugh. "I know, I'm sorry. I'm being ridiculous. You do this for a living. The kids are probably safer with you. Call Nathan's cell if you need us."

"I will. Go. Have fun." Leigh shivered as a cold blast of air scattered the leaves on the front porch. The weather that month had changed drastically in a matter of weeks.

"Okay, I'm going." She slowly made her way to the truck and hesitated at the door.

Nathan pulled her inside and shut the door, yelling, "Go, Luke, go!"

Leigh laughed as she closed the door. Wrapping her sweater tighter around her and grabbing her laptop, she headed into the sitting area. The old stonework fireplace blazed, creating a warm, inviting heat. A corner lamp provided the only source of light in the cozy room as Leigh sat in the rocking chair and propped her feet on the ottoman.

A couple descended the stairs from the guest quarters, dressed as zombies. They waved in greeting as they passed the sitting room on their way out.

"Have a great time," she called, opening the internet connection on her laptop and typing in the Inn's pass code for their Wi-Fi. The high-speed internet was the first upgrade Victoria Mason had introduced as the new co-owner the year before.

Leigh had emailed her mother earlier that day to arrange a time to call and she was nervous about sharing her news. Would they be happy? Supportive at least? It saddened her that she wasn't close enough to them to be sure of a positive reaction. She waited while the computer connected, and then she placed the call to her parents in South Africa. Eight o'clock in Brookhollow meant it was 5:00 a.m. the next day in the remote community where they were stationed until Christmas, but she knew they started their shift at the clinic at six.

"Hello? Leigh?" Her mother's thin face appeared on the blurry screen as she searched the computer for Leigh. "Leigh, you there?"

No matter how many times they did this, her mother still wasn't completely familiar with the process. "Yes, hi, Mom," she said with a wave.

"Leigh, darling, can you see us?" her mother asked, obviously before her delayed response registered on their end, so Leigh didn't respond. Things could get confusing with the slight delay if everyone started talking in the moments of silence.

"How is she?" Her dad appeared on the tiny screen behind her mother.

"Ask her—she's right there," her mother said, moving over to allow him to plaster his face to the screen.

"Leigh?"

"Hi, Dad, you look great," she said, smiling. All she could see of him on the monitor was his forehead.

"How are you, honey? Everything okay?" Usually they waited until Sunday evenings to chat, but she hadn't wanted to wait. "Where are you?"

"I'm great, everything's good. I'm at the B-and-B, babysitting for Rachel and Nathan. The Halloween party at the community hall is tonight."

"You didn't go?" Her mother pushed her father aside and her head appeared in the far right corner of the screen.

"No, not this year." In truth, she hadn't gone since the divorce. Neil had always loved Halloween—really getting into the spirit with over-the-top costumes and transforming their front yard into a grave site and crime scene. Then he would stand in the sunroom wearing a white blanket, a strobe light flashing behind him, pretending to be a ghost for the trick-or-treaters while she handed out candy. Essentially he'd gotten Halloween in the divorce settlement.

"Isn't the party kind of early? They usually hold it the week before Halloween."

"Yes, but Mrs. Dawson is also hosting a murder-mystery party at the hall next week, so..." She didn't want to discuss all of this, but at least it gave her time to stall before sharing her news. She took a deep breath. Like pulling off a Band-Aid: do it quickly. "Anyway, as I mentioned in the email, I have some news I want to share with you both."

The screen lost connection and the image disappeared for a second. *Oh, come on.* She watched the silent circle on the screen processing, trying to reestablish the connection. The internet had the worst timing. This happened when she was trying to tell them about the divorce, as well. Maybe the connection was trying to tell her something, she mused. The connection reopened, and her parents reappeared. They were both leaning over the screen, pressing buttons and bickering.

"I'm back. I'm here." Leigh waved a hand in front of the camera on her laptop.

"There she is," her mother said.

"Okay, Leigh, darling, I have to go. Fill your mom in on the news and she'll tell me all about it," her father said, blowing her a kiss and disappearing.

"No, Dad, wait," she said, but she could see the front door close behind him in the background behind her mother.

"Sorry, his pager was going off—an emergency snakebite victim needed anesthetic. So, what was the good news?'

Leigh hid her disappointment. A snakebite sounded serious, and over the years, traveling with her parents to Third World, impoverished communities, she'd learned compassion for others and how to put the needs of others before herself. She'd also learned from an early age that she would have to accept the limited time her parents could afford her. But she'd really been hoping to tell them both. "Um…I've made an important decision."

"You've decided to do missionary work?" Her mother's eyes lit up.

Great, now any news she had would pale in comparison to that statement. She knew her parents would have loved for her to follow in their well-traveled footprints, helping others. She wished they could see that while it was on a smaller scale, she felt she was helping others with her day care and now with her decision to open her home and her heart to a child. "No, I haven't—"

The sound of creaking on the staircase caught her attention. Glancing up, she met Logan's gaze. She'd assumed he'd be working on new content all evening, though she had been hoping for a glimpse of him.

"Honey, you there?"

"Yes, Mom." She paused as Logan came into the room. "Just Skyping with my parents," she whispered over the laptop monitor.

"Leigh, who are you talking to?"

"A guest at the Brookhollow Inn, Mom. Um…I'll email you later, okay?"

"Oh no, I'll leave—please continue," Logan said, turning to leave.

"I thought you had something important to tell us," her mother said at the same time.

"No!" she called to Logan.

"You don't have something to tell me?" Her mother's confusion was clear.

Logan stopped. "You sure?"

"Yeah, come in, sit. I'll call them later." Then turning to the screen, she said, "It can wait. I'll call you on Sunday night. Give my love to Dad. Take care." In all honesty, she was relieved by Logan's interruption. It gave her an excuse to put this off. Deep down she was nervous about their reaction.

"Okay, darling, hugs and kisses." Her

mother blew her a kiss before the connection disappeared.

Closing her laptop, she smiled at Logan.

"Did you just hang up on your parents?"

Leigh shrugged, knowing that it must have appeared odd. "They had to go, anyway. I'll talk to them later."

"What are you doing here?" he asked.

She picked up the baby monitor. "Babysitting."

"Oh." He glanced around the room.

"They're asleep and the older three are at their aunt's house." Adjusting the volume on the monitor, she set it aside.

"Sounds like an easy night, then." He shoved his hands deep in the pockets of his worn jeans.

"And how about you? How's the writing going?" she asked. After the haunted hike, he'd claimed to be inspired. He'd seemed disappointed when she said she couldn't help him that evening, but he'd claimed to need the time to try to write new content anyway.

"Better." Logan took a seat on the love seat across from her and folded one leg over the other. He leaned against the cushions and ran his good hand through his hair.

Somehow, he made the disheveled look irresistibly tempting. He caught her staring and she glanced away. "That's good," she said.

In the ensuing silence, Logan cleared his throat before saying, "So, your parents aren't here, in Brookhollow?"

"No. They're missionaries. They're never in one place for long. Currently they're in South Africa at a small medical facility. My dad's a doctor, and my mother is trained in first-aid administration."

"That's admirable work. How long have they been doing this?"

"Since before they had me and no, I'm not telling you my age," she said.

He grinned.

"Until I was fifteen, I used to travel with them."

"Wow, interesting childhood." He leaned forward, resting his elbows on his knees as he continued to study her with unconcealed interest.

"Interesting, definitely. Stable, no." She couldn't remember staying in any one place longer than six months. Every move meant a new community, often a new language, a new school, a new set of vaccinations. At fifteen, she hadn't understood her parents' decision to send her to live with Grandma Norris, but now, an adult, and someone wanting a family of her own, she understood the importance of stability for children and over the years, she'd come to appreciate her parents' decision. Even if it had created a gap between them.

Logan nodded. "Moving around can be difficult on a child," he said, his expression clouding over.

She wondered about it. "Have you always lived in New York?" she asked, not willing to let the opportunity to learn more about him pass by.

"No," Logan said, shaking his head. "I was born in California."

"Moved from one coast to the other?"

"And everywhere in between."

"Military family?" The only other family situation she knew of that moved as much as her family did.

"No family."

Her eyebrows rose at the bluntness of

the unexpected answer. She shook her head slowly. "I'm sorry," she mumbled, unsure what else to say.

He shrugged. "Honestly, I don't even know what I'm missing. I was in an orphanage as a baby. Then I was placed in foster homes until I was fifteen and finally decided I'd had enough. I ran away and hitched a ride to New York, stopping along the way and earning money busing tables at truck stops to make it the entire way."

"At fifteen?" She couldn't believe it. At fifteen, she'd stopped traveling to live with her grandmother, but she'd never have been able to do it on her own.

"Yeah. I couldn't take living in the foster homes anymore and I knew I wanted to be a writer."

"So New York was the place to be." She eyed him. He was sharing a lot…a lot more than she would have expected, given how guarded he'd been when they first met. She was curious about his daughter, but she didn't want to push him further than he was comfortable sharing. "So, your series—six books?" Okay, she'd chickened out, keeping to a safer topic—for his sake or hers, she wasn't sure.

"It hadn't started out that way. It had originally been a stand-alone novel, but the fans wanted more of Gardener, so it just kind of spiraled. Then my ex and I separated and there were a few years between books four and the upcoming release next month. Six years, in fact."

"Wow, that's quite a gap."

"Yeah, that's why this comeback needs to be successful." He shifted on the sofa, moving to the edge of the cushion, the look in his eyes suddenly intense. "So, I've been thinking about what you said last night—about the ending."

"Oh, I hope I didn't offend. I really don't know what I'm talking about."

Logan stood and, crossing the room, lifted her legs from the ottoman. Sitting, he placed her legs across his lap. She had trouble focusing on what he said next. "No, you were right. I reread the last few chapters today, and the ending is written all over the page. It's predictable and not the right ending for the book." Was she supposed to be listening? He was gently massaging her feet as he spoke—the cast didn't seem to hinder him when it came to giving foot rubs—and she couldn't remember the last time someone had been this close, this intimate. Did he realize the effect he was having on her? Did he even realize what he was doing? He seemed oblivious as he continued discussing the direction of his novel.

A soft cry came from the monitor on the table next to them and Logan jumped up from the ottoman, allowing Leigh's legs to fall.

Oh, thank God for the interruption. She hadn't heard a word he'd been saying and her brain had turned to mush under his touch. "One of the babies," she mumbled, standing quickly.

Another wail followed.

"And there's the other one. Excuse me for just a few minutes while I get them settled back to sleep." She was both relieved and disappointed by the interruption. Logan's intimate gesture had left her feeling slightly dizzy. Wrapping his arm around her on the haunted hike…then placing her legs on his… Definitely dizzy and excited.

Could he be feeling something happening between them or was he just comfortable around her?

"Need some help?"

That made her wonder how old his daughter was. She hesitated, then nodded. "Sure, thank you." Two crying babies would be a challenge; his help would be appreciated. Her acceptance of his offer had nothing at all to do with wanting to see how he handled a crying baby. Not at all.

At the end of the hall, she opened the bedroom door and smiled at the twins as she entered, and flicked on their butterfly lamp. "Hi, baby girls," she said. "I'll get Abigail if you could get Mackenzie." She gestured to the crib on the other side of the room as she picked up one of the little girls and cradled her in her arms, snug against her chest.

She softly touched Abigail's cheek, watching as Logan gently lifted the second baby, securing her yellow blanket around her. "How do you tell them apart?" he asked, glancing back between the two. Mackenzie snuggled against him and stopped crying immediately.

Though she'd been curious to see it, she hadn't been prepared for the effect the sight Logan holding the baby would have on her. Few men had ever captured her interest, even fewer since her divorce from Neil. But in that tiny gesture, Logan had secured a spot in her heart. He was a natural. So assured and comfortable. She couldn't deny the growing attraction she felt for him.

"Um..." What had he asked? Oh, right, the difference between the babies. "Abby has a tiny freckle on her forehead," she whispered, moving closer to him, pointing out the tiny spot on the baby's skin above her barely visible right eyebrow. "That, and the fact that I know which crib belongs to each baby."

"Cute," Logan said then, glancing at the baby in his arms, he grinned. "Mine's asleep."

"Already?" Leigh leaned over his shoulder. Sure enough, Mackenzie's eyes were closed and her breathing was steady and soft. "You made that look easy," she said, watching him carefully place the baby back in her crib.

"What can I say? I have a way with the ladies." He touched her shoulder as he made his way toward the door. "I'll wait downstairs for you."

Abigail wasn't so eager to fall back to sleep, so Leigh sat in the rocking chair near the window. Rocking the little girl in the dimly lit room, she felt her heart swelling. Her adoption interview was in three days—she could have a baby of her own sooner than she'd thought. Before Christmas…it was too much to hope for. The little girl's eyelids fluttered shut and, careful not to wake her, Leigh placed her back in the crib, tucking a tiny pale pink blanket around her. Tiptoeing out of the room, she closed the bedroom door behind her and made her way down the stairs.

"That was easy," Logan said when she took a seat next to him on the sofa.

"They're really good babies. Rachel and Nathan are fantastic parents and it shows in their children's behavior," she said.

He studied her for a long moment. "Okay, I'm sorry, but I have to ask."

Leigh held her breath, waiting for the

question she'd been asked a hundred times before.

"Why don't you have any of your own? You clearly love them and you would make a terrific mother." Logan turned on the couch to look at her, resting his cast on the back of the love seat.

What else could she tell him, other than the truth? "I can't have children."

He looked down. "I'm so sorry, Leigh. It was none of my business. I shouldn't have asked."

"It's okay. I stopped trying a long time ago, well, obviously since my divorce and I've had a long time to accept it."

He looked back up but remained silent.

"It was also one of the reasons for the divorce," she continued. "The main reason, actually."

Reaching across the love seat, he placed his good hand on top of hers, his eyes never leaving her face.

The reassurance in his firm hold on her hand helped her find the words. "Neil and I got married very young. I was twenty-four, he was twenty-five. We'd been together since high school. Small towns, I guess. Anyway, we started trying to have a baby after our second anniversary. I can still remember the day I found out I was expecting. I was at the grocery store and I must have walked down the aisle with the family-planning products a dozen times, trying to think of excuses to give whoever would check me out at the counter," she said.

"Avoiding small-town gossip is tough, huh?"

"You couldn't possibly understand how hard. Anyway, I stole it." She'd never admitted it to anyone before, not even Neil, and she wasn't sure what made her confess now.

Logan laughed deeply as he squeezed her hand, shaking his head. "You continue to surprise me."

"I know it was awful, but I did donate the money I would have spent on the test to a charity collecting money in the store's entryway as I left," she added quickly.

"I'm sure you properly restored your karma."

"At home, it took me three hours to finally take the test and then I just sat there, staring. When I told Neil, he was ecstatic. He comes from a family of seven brothers and sisters." He was already on his way to having his own big family now, she didn't add.

"What happened?"

"We don't know exactly. I started having contractions at four months, two days after we'd announced the pregnancy to our family and friends. At the hospital, the ultrasound revealed no heartbeat." Her jaw tightened.

Despite the following two miscarriages, that first one had been the hardest and that day at the hospital was one of her worst memories. The fear as they'd driven to the clinic and the sense of urgency and panic the doctors and nurses tried but failed to conceal. Things hadn't been fine; things had been devastating.

Logan's hand tightened around hers again and he moved closer. "I'm sorry, Leigh."

She swallowed hard and cleared her throat before continuing. "After that, there were two more within two years. The doctors ran every test they could think of. We even did DNA testing to see if we were just not compatible…but according to the doctors there was no medical reason they could find to explain why I couldn't carry a baby to term. That was hard to accept." She paused. Without knowing what the problem was, they'd been unable to offer a solution on how to fix it. She looked up from their entwined hands to Logan. His sympathy and concern were too much. "Do you really want to hear all of this?"

"Absolutely," he said.

"Well, after all that, conceiving became difficult, so after a year and a half of no luck, we started the fertility treatments. Nothing worked." She swallowed hard. "And by then, Neil and I had grown so obsessed with having a child, it was all we could think about, talk about. He filed for divorce two weeks after the last round of in vitro failed. So, that's my story."

"It sucks."

Leigh gave a small laugh, blinking back tears. "Yes, it does."

The silence that followed was comforting in a strange way. The only people she'd ever talked about her past failures with were her grandmother and Rachel. Even her parents didn't know the full extent of what she'd been through. She didn't regret telling Logan. She suspected in some way he understood her heartache.

"Amelia is eight."

She knew without asking who Amelia was. "She lives with her mother?"

"For now. I'm hoping to change that." His jaw hardened. "Kendra—my ex," he said in a tight voice, "is an off-Broadway actress who just recently decided that to further her career, she needed to move to L.A. We met on the set of *Women Up,* a play I'd cowritten when I was desperate for money fifteen years ago, before my big break. She lit up the stage with her talent. I was totally taken with her. Amelia was born the same year I signed a contract to sell my first novel. While Kendra traveled with the plays she starred in, I was Amelia's primary caregiver until Kendra fell in love with a costar two years ago and we separated."

"So you share custody of Amelia?"

"We did, until last month when Kendra took Amelia to L.A. with her."

"Oh no, Logan. Is there anything you can do?"

"I'm certainly going to try. We have a court date set for next month and I'm asking for full custody so she can stay in New York with me. Until then, she's in L.A. with her mom."

Leigh wasn't sure which was worse, to never have a child or to have one taken away. "I don't even know what to say Logan," she said softly. He would have a fight on his hands, she knew that for sure, and her heart ached for him.

"That's why this book, this comeback is so important. I need the courts to see that I can continue to support Amelia."

"Don't worry. You'll finish the series and it'll be wonderful." She touched the side of his cheek. Her fingers moved along his strong jawline, and he turned his face to kiss the palm of her hand.

She swallowed a lump in her throat as their gazes met and she leaned in for the kiss on the lips she knew was coming.

Gently he took her by the shoulders, the move made more awkward by his cast. He studied her face. "I can't, Leigh. I wish I could, but…I had a home, my only home, with Amelia and Kendra. I need to know I can have that again with my daughter. If I can't…"

Slowly he let his hands fall away from her as he put distance between them on the sofa.

"If I can't," he said softly, "I don't think I could trust making a new life with anyone else again."

CHAPTER SIX

"WHERE ARE WE putting this set of lights?" Dylan asked, tangled in a set of pumpkin lanterns on the far end of the front yard.

Leigh looked up from where she was tying a stuffed plastic bag ghost to a post on her fence. Good question. Decorating their front yard for Halloween had been Neil's thing. She'd almost forgotten all of these decorations were still in her garage. "Um…" Where had he usually hung them?

"Miss Leigh, the inflatable vampire in the coffin keeps floating away in the wind," Melissa said, desperately battling to hold the inflatable eight-foot-wide lawn ornament in place by lying on it.

"That's because we need to secure it to the ground." Allowing the end of the ghost to fly free, she went to help the child. "There should have been plastic spikes in the box." She scanned the front yard. Shoot, they must have left the box in the garage.

"Miss Leigh, where should I put this pumpkin?" Isabel asked from the deck where she stood holding a pumpkin almost as big as her tiny body. "Quick, it's getting heavy." The pumpkin started to slip out of the girl's fingers.

Rushing toward her, she caught the pumpkin before it could hit the deck. That was one mess she didn't want to have to clean up before the adoption caseworker arrived that evening. Butterflies developed in the pit of her stomach at the thought of her evening appointment. Friday night, sharing stories of their past with Logan, she'd almost forgotten about her home visit that evening, but that morning, it had been the first thought she'd had upon opening her eyes. She wanted to make a good impression…needed to.

"What about the lights?" Dylan asked again as Leigh positioned the pumpkin, carved face out, on the top step.

Maybe involving kids this age in decorating the yard hadn't been such a great idea. She should have at least waited until a day when Ashley could help. But she'd really wanted Michelle Bennett to see her home decorated for the season. At least she hoped celebrating Halloween would be seen as a positive thing. She scanned the yard. Maybe this wasn't such a great idea, after all. Well, it was too late now. There was no way she could tell these eager-to-help children to stop decorating.

"Miss Leigh, help!" Melissa yelled before the vinyl fabric swallowed her and she disappeared in the rolls of the inflated coffin.

"I got it," said a man with a deep voice to her left.

Turning, she saw Logan run through the gate to Melissa's aid. A memory of their hands intertwined flashed in her mind and she felt her cheeks grow warm despite the violent cool breeze.

He couldn't make a home with her—with anyone—unless he got his child back. She had to accept that.

"Thanks," Melissa said, admiring her rescuer. "You saved me."

Great, the girl believed in fairy tales already. "Thank you, Logan," Leigh said, taking Melissa out of his arms and setting her on the lawn. "Why don't you go help Dylan with those lights?" she said to the child.

"I'd rather help Mr. Walters."

Who wouldn't? The dreamy look on Melissa's face made Leigh wonder if that was how she looked at Logan when he wasn't paying attention. "Go." Leigh pointed across the yard.

"Okay." Melissa reluctantly went to help the little boy with the tangled lights.

"Were you out of your mind trying to do this with a group of four-year-olds?" Logan asked, surveying the disaster.

"Probably, certainly in hindsight it looks that way. A few more full-size hands would definitely be appreciated," Leigh said with a laugh.

"I've got *one* if that helps."

"Shouldn't you be trying to write with that one hand?" Not that she didn't want his help. It was just that she was very aware that she was getting too close to him for her own good. The man had said he couldn't build a home with her. It made her growing attraction to him more than inconvenient. She didn't want to put herself through the pain of another man she cared for walking out on her. He'd as good as told her he would.

Working together on his book was going to be exceedingly difficult for her after his admission the other night.

"I've done quite a bit today already and you're not available tonight, so I can always work on it again later." He scanned the yard, rolling up the sleeves of his dark blue fleece jacket. "Where can I start?"

"Well, if you're sure…the spikes for that coffin should be in the box in the garage, just around the corner."

"Great."

While she waited, she sat on the inflatable decoration to prevent it from flying into the backyard of the bed-and-breakfast and watched as Dylan, Melissa and Isabel untangled the pumpkin lights and began draping them over the fence. Exactly where Neil had hung them year after year. "Looks great, guys."

"Here they are," Logan said, returning with the four plastic spikes.

"Perfect. If you want to just make sure this thing doesn't blow away, I'll secure it to the ground." She accepted his hand for help up and couldn't help noticing how warm and strong it felt wrapped around her cold one. She'd experienced the same feelings Friday night when his reassuring touch had given her the courage to tell him about her past. Letting go of his hand, she took the first spike and pushed it through the loop in the fabric and into the grass.

"So, big plans for tonight?"

Logan's question caught her off guard and she hesitated. Yes, huge plans…none of which she wanted to reveal. "Um… just meeting with a friend." She'd spoken to Michelle twice on the phone…okay… maybe *friend* was a stretch, but she suspected at the end of this emotional process, she would be able to call the woman a close acquaintance at least.

"A boyfriend?" Dylan asked from behind her.

Where had he come from? Leigh drove the last spike in the ground and ruffled the boy's hair. "No. Not a boyfriend."

"That's good," the little boy and the man said simultaneously.

Leigh's surprised expression met Logan's sheepish one.

"Guess I'm not the only one who has a crush on Miss Leigh," he whispered.

That would be wonderful, she thought, if he hadn't confessed that he wouldn't let himself act on his feelings.

LEIGH PACED HER living room, checking everything for the hundredth time. The children's toys were sorted and neatly placed in stacking bins along the toy shelf. Their books and puzzles were lined up according to size on the small plastic bookshelf. All of their cups and plates were still sitting in the dish rack on the kitchen counter. They were dry already, but she'd read somewhere that allowing dishes to dry on their own was a more sanitary approach to cleaning and she wanted to display her knowledge, however small, to Michelle.

She sniffed the air. Was the smell of the floor cleanser too strong? Maybe she should put away the dishes. She bit her lip; the nervous flutter in her stomach persisted. What if this woman found something she didn't like? Her house was comfortable, but it was far from big. But it was definitely safe…childproof…security gate at the top of the stairs leading to the unfinished basement, outlet covers, dead bolt on the front door, kitchen cabinet and door stoppers. Was she missing something?

She heard a car pull into her driveway and said a silent prayer as she watched a young woman in a dark coat, belted at the waist, a bright yellow scarf wrapped around her neck, make her way to the front door. Leigh quickly released the living-room curtain and hurried to the door.

With a shaking hand, she unlocked the dead bolt and forced a smile before opening the front door. On the other side, the woman was scanning the decorated yard. "Hi. Ms. Bennett?"

"Leigh, a pleasure to meet you," the woman said. "Great decorations—your day-care children helped?"

Leigh laughed. "How could you tell?" She moved back to let the woman in, offering to take her coat.

"What a beautiful home you have," she said, handing Leigh her coat.

Leigh's gaze immediately fell to the tiny bulge visible under the woman's loose-fitting top above her dress pants. Undeniably, the beginning of a baby bump. Some days it honestly felt like everyone was pregnant…everyone but her. She pushed away a slight pang of jealousy as she said, "Thank you."

"And I must say, so far, I'm impressed with the neighborhood and Brookhollow in general. This is the first time I've been here."

"Thank you, yes, Brookhollow is an amazing place to live…and raise a family," she added, leading the way into the kitchen. "Would you like tea, coffee?" she asked, as the woman made notes on the state of the home.

"Tea would be great, thank you. Where's the best place to set up?" she asked.

"The living room is probably the most comfortable or the sitting room out front."

A few moments later, tea in hand, she joined Michelle in the sitting room, where the social worker had opened her briefcase and removed the necessary paperwork. Placing their tea on the table, Leigh took a seat in her favorite armchair, across from the person who held her fate in her decision.

But Michelle's face was pale as she rummaged in her purse.

"You okay?"

She sighed. "Yes…I'm sorry. This is embarrassing…but I'm nauseous and I can't find my soda crackers…"

Leigh offered a sympathetic smile. She may not have been able to carry a baby to term, but she'd always been pregnant just long enough to experience the nausea. "Just a sec."

When she returned, she handed her a bag of Cheerios. "Try these."

"Cheerios?"

"They work like a charm."

Michelle took the bag and tossed a handful into her mouth. "Thank you. Pretty soon, I won't be conducting these home visits…it can get a little uncomfortable. I hope you are okay with my insistence on being the one to meet with you today—I just felt we had a great rapport."

"It's fine, really." What choice did she have? She wanted this adoption process to go smoothly and she would rather continue communicating with Michelle than to start over with a stranger.

"Should we begin?" she asked.

"Yes, please." Leigh leaned forward in her chair, folding her shaking hands over her knees. The mix of emotions erupting inside her was almost too much. This had to go well.

"Well, first, I'd love to hear about your own childhood. I've read your application, but I'd love to know more. Your parents are missionaries?"

"Yes, my father is a doctor and he was working with Doctors Without Borders in New York immediately after his residency at New York University Hospital. He's always known that he wanted to work abroad in countries where the medical care was less than adequate. That's also how my parents met. My mother was assigned to the same group on her first trip to South Africa as an administration assistant. I was born here in Brookhollow, but only barely. I arrived three days early and my parents were on their way back from Bosnia when she went into labor on the flight."

Michelle's eyes widened. "Oh no! How terrifying."

"Luckily, they were only an hour outside Newark."

"That *was* lucky," Michelle said with a nod. "I can only imagine how awful it would be to deliver a baby on a plane—for everyone," she added with a laugh. "And you are an only child?" She scanned her file. "After a scare like that, I can't say I blame them for stopping at one."

"Yes. Actually I'm not sure my parents ever really planned to have *any* children. I just sort of happened."

"So, then you accompanied them on these mission trips around the world?"

"My first station was when I was less than six months old. As soon as the doctors said I was old enough to receive the travel vaccinations, my parents returned to the field."

"Wow, that's a unique childhood."

From Michelle's tone, Leigh couldn't decide if she meant *good* unique or *bad* unique, and she was unable to read the notes the woman made on the application form on her lap, so she remained silent. Michelle leafed through the papers in her file. "And at fifteen, you moved in with your grandmother?"

"Yes. My parents decided that I should go to high school with my cousins and friends here. I'd been homeschooled by my mom while we traveled."

"And how was attending a regular school?" she tossed another handful of Cheerios into her mouth.

"Honestly? Boring," Leigh said with a laugh. "My mother had been teaching me curriculum far above my grade level, so the classes weren't challenging enough, but I did graduate top of the class my senior year and the socializing was exactly what I'd been missing." She never would have experienced normal teenage stuff had her parents not made the decision they had. She never would have attended prom…or met Neil and fallen in love. She'd missed her parents, but their relationship hadn't been typical from the start. They'd never felt as much like a family unit, as a team that functioned well together.

"And living with your grandmother? How was that?"

"Wonderful. We're a lot alike, and by then my grandfather had passed away, so it was just us. We lived in her two-bedroom apartment above her bakery on Main Street. I worked there every day before and after school."

"I thought I smelled baked goods coming from your kitchen." Michelle looked hopeful.

"I made a pumpkin-spiced loaf this afternoon. Would you like a piece?" If baked goods were the way to securing a high score on Michelle's placement analysis, she had nothing to worry about.

"Definitely, maybe before we do the house tour. Shall we move on with the rest of the questions first?"

Leigh nodded, taking a sip of her tea.

"Your marital status…" She scanned the application.

"Divorced."

"Right, for four years now?"

"Almost five." They were coming up on the anniversary of the divorce the following week. Each year, despite her best efforts to forget what day it was, the reminder was the first thing that popped into her mind upon waking, every October twenty-third. She couldn't help feeling a little sad on the anniversary of their divorce, but each year it got a little easier.

"And he is…still living here in Brookhollow?"

"With his new wife and two children."

The woman studied her. "In a town this size, I imagine that can be difficult. But you've learned to accept that and move on?"

Leigh took a moment to respond. Had she? She felt fine…most days. Sure, running into Neil and his new family wasn't the most pleasant situation, especially when Angela seemed to always be pregnant, but the intense pain she'd felt at one time had subsided over the years to more of a dull disappointment and a feeling of loss over what could have been.

Of course, she was still hiding from the woman at every opportunity. Did that mean she hadn't moved on?

Finally she said, "I don't think anyone ever fully recovers from a failed marriage, but I think I've had enough time to move past the hurt. It certainly doesn't affect my day-to-day life and as they say, time heals."

Michelle seemed satisfied with her response and nodded. "With regards to raising a child, do you think you would like to raise your own children the way your parents did? Or will you be staying in Brookhollow?"

"As much as I learned from traveling, I feel that I missed out on a lot. I believe children need stability. Brookhollow is home and always will be, so other than vacations, I can't see home being anywhere else but here."

"That's important, as you have decided to go with an open adoption, which means the birth mother will have certain accessibility rights to the child. We hesitate to place children in this type of adoption with families where there's a potential to relocate."

"I understand." Moving was not an option and that was fine with her. She didn't want to be anywhere else. She sympathized with Logan's dilemma. If he lost his court case, he'd be forced to move.

"What about your parents' discipline style? Were they lenient or authoritative, and would you say you would model their example?"

"My mom was the disciplinarian in our home—wherever it was at the moment—as my father was usually far too exhausted after fourteen- to sixteen-hour shifts at the medical clinics. Punishments usually included housework or loss of privileges. Not that there were many of those to begin with. A television was a luxury in most places. My parents didn't believe in physical discipline and neither do I. I can definitely see myself mirroring my mother's techniques for sure. She always made sure I knew right from wrong and that there were consequences to my decisions and actions."

Her parents had never left any doubt in her mind that she was loved and cared for, including how they approached raising her to be the best person she could be. They were good people, probably better than most, given their selfless nature and career choice, and she liked to believe their charity and kindness had been passed along to her.

Michelle's expression was unreadable as she studied her in silence. Crap, had she said something wrong? "Michelle?"

The woman cleared her throat. "Sorry. I…uh…" She swallowed hard and coughed again. Setting the file aside, she took a sip of her tea. "It's just that every time I meet with adoptive parents, they always seem so confident, so sure."

Wow, if only this woman could hear the doubts that plagued her. She was glad they weren't showing, however.

"They have everything planned. They are ready."

"Well, in my case, I've been trying for so long, I am ready."

"I wish I was as confident."

"You still have time…you will be." When had the roles changed?

Michelle shook her head, picking up the file. "Sorry for the minor meltdown. Let's get back to you," she said with a laugh. "So far, everything sounds great. Um…let's talk about relationships. On your application you stated you were adopting alone. Is that still the case?"

"Yes. There is no one significant in my life." An image of Logan flashed in her mind and she frowned. Logan wasn't significant. He was…what? The only man in a long time she'd felt a genuine connection with, the first person in a long time she thought might truly understand some of the things she was dealing with and going through… The only man ever to get her heart racing with a simple look or touch? Okay, maybe he *was* significant, but he was also not offering her a future.

"Well, that's certainly not a problem for the process. I just want you to keep in mind the type of relationships you will have going forward. You will be a family with this child, and your future decisions about who you bring into your lives will affect the child, as well. The way you think of relationships and men will change… and so will your availability—both physically and emotionally. We find in situations like this that the parent and the child form a bond in the years they are alone and it often creates a situation where the new parent feels a bit like an outsider. How would you deal with a situation like that?" she asked, pen poised above her paper.

The questions had suddenly gotten harder. She didn't see the possibility of a relationship in her near future, but it was something she obviously needed to consider…at least for the sake of this interview. "I guess, as you said, my idea of relationships will change and I would be looking for not only a good husband, but also a good father…someone who loves children…has a good idea of family and what it means." No doubt finding someone who would embrace her situation would be difficult. "And honestly, Michelle, I'm fully prepared to raise a child on my own. I'm not currently looking for or hoping for a change in relationship status."

Michelle smiled. "But we can never say never, right? Life happens beyond our control sometimes, so it's just something we like all of our applicants to seriously take time to consider, as it affects everyone involved with this process—you, your baby and the birth mother." She paused. "Okay.

Another difficult question, and if you need to take a moment to give it some thought, please do." Michelle's voice was gentle as she put the paper aside. "There is the concern over your own fertility and whether or not you have grieved sufficiently over your inability to have a child of your own. Do you think you're ready to abandon those avenues? It's not to say that you couldn't adopt and then someday have a child of your own...it's just something we need to consider."

Leigh had to wipe away tears.

"Sorry if that topic upsets you," Michelle said, reaching for her paper.

Leigh held out a hand to stop her. "Not for the reason you may think. I'm overwhelmed by your agency's commitment to finding the best possible homes for these children. I've known for a long time that having my own child wasn't an option and I've come to terms with that. Trying for a baby of my own dominated a lot of my life and ultimately ruined my marriage, so I have put that possibility aside permanently. I'm not prepared to put myself or anyone else through that heartache anymore. Yet I have a lot of love to offer a child, given the opportunity."

Michelle touched Leigh's hand. "That's what I wanted to hear." She leaned back in her chair and took a sip of her tea. "So, as I mentioned on the phone, this process could still take a while. We are now going to review your letters of recommendation and we may call a few of your references... but as far as I'm concerned, you've passed the home-study interview."

Overwhelmed with relief and happiness, Leigh sighed. "Thank you."

"Let me tell you about the possible candidate."

Leigh swallowed hard, fisting her hands on her lap. *Don't get too excited...not yet.* The word *may* hadn't escaped her notice.

"There's a young woman in our system due to deliver in two weeks. She placed the request for this home study after reviewing your file. Yours and one other."

"What does that mean?"

"Well, after we complete the second home study, we provide her with our findings and offer our suggestions on the best fit. Ultimately in an open adoption like this, the decision is hers."

"Will I meet her?" The idea was both terrifying and exhilarating. By Thanksgiving, she could have a child of her own...*if* this woman chose her.

"Only after she makes a decision based on the paperwork and our recommendations. We don't believe in raising the adoptive parent's hopes, only to disappoint them. As I said, she is considering two separate files and there is the chance that she will select the other applicant. Either way, we should have an answer for you by the end of the week."

Friday suddenly seemed a million years away. "That sounds wonderful."

"Oh, but I can give you this," Michelle said, handing her a folder. "This is information about the birth mother, as much as we're permitted to disclose at this time, in case you have any questions or concerns."

Leigh clutched the file to her chest. Information about the birth mother of a baby that could potentially be hers was inside.

She couldn't wait to open it.

FROM HIS WINDOW at the bed-and-breakfast, Logan could see a thin, young woman leaving Leigh's house next door about an hour after she had gone inside. He couldn't help feeling like a stalker, but he also couldn't help feeling relieved that Leigh had been telling the truth about her evening plans. And then there was the nagging curiosity plaguing him and the tiny voice in the back of his mind reminding him that he wasn't even supposed to care. The problem was that he did care. A lot. And yet he'd already started to look for homes in L.A. He'd been serious when he told Leigh that if he couldn't have his home back with his daughter, he didn't want to risk building a home with anyone else ever again. The hurt was too great.

His cell phone rang on the desk, and Clive's number lit up the display. He contemplated ignoring it, but the man deserved an update at least. "Hey, Clive," he said, taking the call.

"Tell me you're making progress."

"I'm making progress." Sort of. Maybe progress in the wrong direction, but it was still progress right?

"Really?"

"Yeah. I…uh…hired a typist."

"You're lying."

"No, really I did." They hadn't exactly talked payment, except for his brief mention of it at the haunted hike, but he certainly planned on compensating Leigh. Of course, he'd rather show her his gratitude in other ways like taking her out on a real date, telling her how wonderful she was and helping to erase some of the pain in her past. But he wouldn't allow himself too tempting a prospect of a future with her.

"From what agency?" Clive asked suspiciously.

"No agency. She's just a woman who lives here, next door to the B-and-B." It was such an understatement of who Leigh was that Logan was almost embarrassed by the lie. But what could he tell Clive? That he was getting help from a woman he would not let himself fall in love with in the small town?

"Not the same woman who pushed you off a ladder?"

"Actually yes."

Clive laughed. "Wow, way to call in the guilt favor."

Logan moved away from the window and sat in the desk chair. He knew that was exactly how Leigh had gotten wrapped up in this. Her guilt over his injury had certainly been the only logical explanation for her agreeing to help, but he hoped there was more to it now. They'd grown so close in the matter of a week. If he hadn't been experiencing it, he'd never have believed it was possible to have a connection this strong to a woman he'd known for such a short period of time. "I'm getting it done, aren't I?"

"Yes, and really that's all I care about. Oh, and of course that it's great."

"Now you're pushing it."

"It will be great. You owe it to your loyal fans."

Logan sighed. "Now who's using the guilt card?"

CHAPTER SEVEN

DESPITE HIS CONVERSATION with Clive the night before, Logan was feeling more productive than he had felt in a long time the next morning as he scribbled the last few lines of a scene, trying to ignore the ache in his hand and his growling stomach. He was getting somewhere. Whenever he thought of the final chapter, he still wasn't convinced it was the right way to end the series, but with a deadline a week away, he needed to push through with the original idea, unless by some miracle another one came to him. He was just thrilled to be writing. Cringing, as he jotted down the last word, he dropped his pen and gripped his aching fingers sticking from the end of the cast. He smiled despite the pain.

His stomach demanded attention and he stood. He'd woken early to start writing the scene that had come to him in his half-awake state, and it was now only a little past eight. The bed-and-breakfast served a hot meal until nine, and the smell of bacon and toast drifting upstairs from the dining room below was mouthwatering. Running a hand through his disheveled hair, he went into the bathroom and splashed hot water on his face, before heading downstairs.

"But Luke was the murderer," he heard a woman say in the dining area. She was clearly distraught.

Murderer? There was a murder in the small town? When? Where? And as he was an outsider, would he be a prime suspect? Man, he had to start writing something other than mysteries. He glanced at the stack of *Brookhollow View,* the town newspaper, on the front reception desk as he passed. The incident hadn't made headlines either. Instead the front-page story was about the results of a dispute that had occurred the night before at the local bingo hall. He picked up a copy. *This* he had to read.

As he peered into the dining room, it

seemed the only one in a panic was a thin, blond, older woman.

"I know, Darlene, but he's stuck in Boston. There's no way he can make it back in time," Victoria was saying as she delivered plates of food to the table in the corner near the front window.

The other woman followed her. "What are we supposed to do now?"

"Can't someone else play the part?" Victoria waved to him as he took a seat at a smaller table near the kitchen door.

"The characters have all been assigned already. That son of mine..."

Victoria held a finger to indicate she'd be a moment longer, before turning to face the woman who was presumably her mother-in-law. "Darlene, you knew when you assigned such an important role to him that he travels outside Brookhollow for work. I know he told you this was a possibility. In fact, I'm pretty positive that he said he wasn't available." He read the exasperation in her green eyes as she made her way to him, mouthing the words *Oh my God,* her hands clenched at her sides.

The older woman stood pouting for a

second before continuing to follow her. "Okay, let's put our heads together. Who wasn't originally invited? Preferably male…"

Victoria let out a deep breath and ignored her as she asked, "What can I get you, Mr. Walters?"

"It's Logan. The breakfast special smells wonderful…. I also wanted to say I'm sorry about how I acted…before…when I first arrived." This was the first chance he'd gotten to say it. The petite blonde always seemed incredibly busy.

"Apology accepted. We all have our moments," she said, darting a look at the older woman, who was inspecting him. "Your breakfast will be out shortly."

"No rush," he said, reaching for his *Brookhollow View* on the table, trying to ignore the way the older woman still studied him. A large advertisement for a murder-mystery party in town that evening at the community hall caught his eye. So that's what this was about.

"I don't believe we've met," the older woman said, moving closer.

"Please don't bother the guests, Darlene," Victoria said as Darlene sat in the wicker chair across from him.

"Logan Walters." He extended his good hand to the woman. If he had to guess, he would have said she was in her early fifties, but he knew if she was Victoria's mother-in-law, she must be quite a bit older. She hid her age well.

"I'm Darlene Dawson, president of the Brookhollow Social Committee. I plan and organize almost all of the events for the community." She folded one long leg over the other and straightened her fashionable pencil skirt.

"Pleasure," Logan said.

"You'll be rethinking that in a minute," Victoria mumbled loud enough for him to hear as she escaped into the kitchen.

"What brings you to Brookhollow, Logan?" Darlene asked.

"Just needed a quiet place to get some work done," he said as Victoria returned with his coffee and placed it on the table in front of him. "Thank you."

"I'd love a coffee as well, Victoria."

"Oh, Darlene, I'm sure Mr. Walters would appreciate being left to have his breakfast alone." She gave the woman a warning look.

"Nonsense, no one likes to eat alone."

"It's okay," Logan said, enjoying the interaction between the two women. Since his arrival at the bed-and-breakfast, Victoria's demeanor had been nothing but professional and friendly, but now with her mother-in-law, she was clearly frazzled.

"Don't say I didn't try," she said as she grabbed an empty cup from the table behind her and filled it with coffee for her mother-in-law.

"So, Logan, what do you do?"

"I'm a writer," he said, noticing too late Victoria shaking her head behind Darlene.

"How fascinating. What kind of books do you write?" She leaned forward on the table.

"I write mysteries."

A wide smile spread across the woman's face and, if possible, she looked even younger. "Well, isn't that just perfect? I'm sure you overheard the conversation I was just having with Victoria. It turns out that we are without a murderer for tomorrow night's murder-mystery party at the community hall." She pointed to the ad on the paper.

Victoria had been right; he should have insisted on dining alone. "Oh, I'm sorry, Darlene. I'd like to help, but I'm on a deadline."

She looked at his cast and arched one thinly curved eyebrow.

"I know how it looks, but I really am here to work."

"It's just a few hours. Surely you could use a break, no pun intended," she said with a light laugh.

"Um..." Why was it that words seemed to depart him at the worst possible times?

Darlene stood and pointed to the advertisement again. "Here is all the information you need. Upon arrival, I will hand out the scripts. Oh, and you wouldn't happen to have a suit with you by any chance?"

"No, I..." Had he agreed already?

"No matter, just wear a dress shirt and tie. That will be fine."

"Oh, but—"

"Thanks a million. You're really helping us out." With a quick turn and small wave, she was gone.

Mouth agape, Logan sat staring after her.

Reappearing with his breakfast, Victoria set the plate on the table in front of him. "I tried to warn you," she said.

WHILE THE KIDS took their afternoon nap, Leigh wandered down the hall to the last bedroom on the right, the one across from her own. Opening the door for only the second time in over four years, she entered what had been meant to be the nursery. A dark mahogany crib was pulled away from the wall in the corner of the room, its sleigh bed design covered in a thin veil of dust. Several yellow paint cans sat on an old bedsheet on the floor beside it. The matching dresser and change table lay in pieces, waiting to be assembled. In the open closet still hung pink and purple baby girl clothing sets and dresses—all for the child she'd lost.

She picked up a butterfly mobile from the top of one of the many boxes and touched one delicate crystal-blue wing. A soft lullaby played in the otherwise silent house as the butterfly wings flapped slowly and the mobile spun. Reaching for a large stuffed baby-elephant toy, she sat in the plush rocking chair in the middle of the room. She closed her eyes as she propped her feet up on the swaying, matching ottoman.

As she'd expected, memories of those excitement-filled afternoons spent planning the baby's room with Neil came flooding back. Three months pregnant, and her wish had been his command. She'd wanted yellow for the walls and three attempts later, he brought home the perfect shade. She'd refused to consider his sisters' secondhand crib sets, wanting her baby to have the best and safest. It seemed as if every other day, Neil came home from work with new clothes to hang in the closet, and the best surprise had been the rocking chair, where she now sat. He'd covered her eyes as he led her down the hall where he'd spent the afternoon putting it together for her. Tears of joy had been the only ones she'd known back then.

She allowed the memories to linger just a fraction longer, before she released them with a deep breath. She'd moved on. She'd let go of the past. Now this room represented something new, something different. A new chapter in her life that was equally exciting.

The ringing of the telephone in the hallway made her jump, and rushing out of the room, she closed the door softly behind her before answering on the third ring, hoping the sound hadn't woken any of the children. "Hello," she whispered, glancing into the playroom's designated nap area. All six kids still slept like little angels on their padded mats, curled up with their favorite stuffed animals.

"Leigh? I can barely hear you."

She recognized the voice immediately, and rushed into the kitchen. "Hi, Michelle. Sorry, the children are napping."

"Oh, sorry, I hope I didn't wake them," the woman said.

"Not at all." Leigh held her breath. *Please have good news.* It was only Tuesday. Michelle had said she would hear something by Friday. Before, early news was good news. She hoped it was the case this time, as well.

"I have news," she said.

News—that didn't help.

"The young mother I mentioned to you said Brookhollow sounds like a lovely place to raise a child and she's impressed by your experience with children, operating a day care and all."

Life-altering news. Too choked up to speak, she managed to squeak out an "okay" before Michelle continued.

"She would really like to meet both families before making her final decision. I know, I said we usually don't allow this—"

"It's fine," Leigh said quickly. "I'll do it." At this point she would do whatever it took. If the young woman wanted to meet her to feel more confident in her decision to choose her, she would readily comply. Heck, if the young woman asked for anything, no request would be unreasonable. After all, she was deciding the fate of her child. She deserved the right to make the most informed decision possible.

"You're sure? As I said, there's no guarantee."

"Michelle, I'm sure. Nothing in life is guaranteed, but you certainly won't succeed if you don't try, right?" Her heart might break if after their meeting, this young woman chose the other parent.

But that was a chance she had to take.

"I CAN'T BELIEVE you were able to get so much done with your hand in that cast," Leigh said, leafing through Logan's work that evening. Sure, it was impossible to read—more so than usual—but there were at least five chapters to add. She wasn't sure, but she suspected it was almost reaching the end. The thought saddened her. She would miss him. She couldn't help wishing he wasn't heading back to the city, but then he had to win custody of his daughter and she wouldn't want to take that away from him. If he didn't win custody, though, and had to move to California and cobble a makeshift life with Amelia, she didn't know if he'd ever trust anyone enough to love them.

"Me, neither. I'm not sure I'm completely happy with the overall direction the book is heading in, but at least I have something to work with now. Better to have words to delete than no words at all." Logan stood and stretched.

"Great motto." They'd been working for two hours and Leigh suppressed a yawn. "Need a break?" she asked.

"Tempting…but no, let's keep going. There are really only a few scenes left for tonight," he said, scanning what was left. "Where are we on word count?"

"Eighty-three thousand and fifty-four words." Wow, she couldn't imagine writing that much.

"Great. We're on track to hit the ninety-thousand mark," he said, sitting back on the bench next to her. "The faster we get this done, the faster you'll be rid of me and have your evenings back."

The realization that he was right hit her with an unexpected anxiety. When he first asked for her help, she'd dreaded giving up her personal time, but now she wasn't looking forward to the quiet, lonely evenings. She shook the thought away. *Think about the baby.* Hopefully soon there would be a new addition to her life. Lonely would no longer be an option. "Thank God," she said, but her attempt to tease failed when her gaze met his.

"I'm going to miss this, too," Logan said,

touching her cheek, quickly, softly, before returning to the work. “Okay, ready?”

The moment was gone and an incredible wave of disappointment cascaded over her. *Get a grip.* There shouldn’t even have been a moment. Lately, there seemed to be too many moments and unfortunately they were a cruel tease of what couldn’t be.

“Ready,” she said, but as she typed the words he dictated, she grew fidgety. She bit her bottom lip, fighting the urge to share her thoughts with him. This was his book—*just type. Just type....*

She stopped typing. “Logan, are you sure this is the way you want this to go?” The detective was about to walk straight into his own demise, and while she hadn’t even read the entire series, even *she* wasn’t happy about it. His faithful fans were going to be disappointed.

“No, I’m not.” He raked a hand through his hair. “But I’ve got one week.” He frowned and his own hesitancy was written all over his face.

“But your fans—”

“Will be disappointed that he dies.”

"And not to mention how they'll feel about him leaving Piper."

Logan frowned. "Okay, now you've lost me."

"Well, I just mean the obvious connection between Van and Piper, the chemistry. They're perfect for each other. And the fans—"

Logan held up a hand. "They're just partners."

Leigh's mouth fell open. "You mean you didn't do it on purpose?"

"Do what?"

"Are you serious?" His silent bewilderment suggested he was. "Logan, you've created a romance behind the mystery. You do realize that, right?" How on earth could he not see the attraction between the detective and his partner? These were characters he'd created and yet he hadn't purposely developed this secondary story line? She'd only read half of the first two books and part of this last one and it was evident to her.

"You're crazy. Piper is just his sidekick."

"A sidekick who *adores* him. Come on, Logan." She scrolled back to one of the first scenes she'd helped him with. "Right here, when she's bandaging his gunshot wound, chemistry…a lot of chemistry…" She scrolled. "And here when she isn't sure if he was in the burning vehicle. These are distraught tears of someone in love, not just a partner."

"I don't know, Leigh. I think you might be imagining it."

"He calls her *baby girl* throughout the book."

"He does that in every book, a little sister affection."

Leigh shuddered. "Granted, I didn't grow up with a brother, but I'm pretty sure if I had one he wouldn't refer to me that intimately. Logan, these two characters love each other."

"Are you sure?" Taking the laptop from her, he searched the page.

"No! I'm definitely not sure, seeing as how these are *your* characters, not mine. But, trust me, if these two don't belong together, no one does."

Logan let out a deep sigh. "So what you're saying is, if I kill Van Gardener, fans are going to hunt me down."

"I'd hire a bodyguard."

Logan laughed and reaching across, he tucked a stray dark strand of hair behind her ear, letting his hand cup the side of her face. "You wouldn't be looking to make a career change, would you?"

The flirting between them was wrong, dangerous and ultimately leading nowhere. It had to stop. Turning her head, she moved out of his reach. "Well, what are you going to do?"

"I have no idea, but I know what I'm *not* going to do," he said, crumpling the last stack of handwritten pages.

"Kill Van Gardener?"

"You got it." He stood. "Well, I guess that means we should stop for tonight. No sense going any further until I figure out how the book ends."

Leigh checked her watch. Just after eight. She was disappointed to have the night end so soon. She had plenty of work to do on the nursery to occupy her time, a nagging voice said. She forced it away. She'd have plenty of time when Logan left as well. She hesitated a second longer, then asked, "Did you want to go grab a coffee?"

The invite was totally transparent, considering she always had coffee with her in her Thermos and they'd consumed copious amounts already that evening.

"Any more coffee and we'll both be buzzing, but don't worry, I wasn't planning to let you go just yet."

She was grateful for the dim lighting inside the gazebo as she felt her cheeks grow hot. But the realization that he didn't want the night to end just yet, either, eased her embarrassment.

"I need to get to a clothing store. Is anything still open around here?" he asked, sliding his laptop into the case.

"The mall stores are open until ten tonight. What do you need?" she asked before she could register that it was none of her business. After all, hadn't he implied that he wanted her to come along?

"A dress shirt and tie. I didn't exactly pack anything dressy before leaving the city, but apparently I somehow agreed to attend that murder-mystery party at the community hall tomorrow night." Logan tossed the bag over his shoulder.

"You met Mrs. Dawson, I take it." Leigh

laughed. That woman could convince anyone to do anything.

"Don't laugh. I'm taking you with me."

"No, I don't think so."

"It's too late to come up with an excuse. Besides, normally you'd be helping me tomorrow evening anyway, so I know you're free."

He had a point. But after their last outing, she suspected rumors were already spreading through town quickly. She didn't need the attention on herself, especially inaccurate gossip about a possible relationship, not when she was hoping to adopt a child.

"Come on, Leigh." He rubbed her arm affectionately, a puppy dog look on his handsome face. "After all, you did push me off a ladder."

"Fine," she said with a sigh. "But that's the last time you can use that one."

"Deal."

"Okay, let's go." She stopped and stared at his unruly hair and more-than-a-little-scruffy beard. Then taking out her phone, she dialed the number to Klip and Dye, the only hair salon in town.

"Who are you calling?"

"Someone who can clean you up a little."

THE BROOKVIEW SQUARE MALL in the town square was practically empty at that time of night and once again Logan couldn't believe just how quiet everything was in the town. In the city, things were fast-paced and alive at any time of day and night. Growing up in California had been the same. He wasn't used to the slow pace or quiet of Brookhollow, but he was certainly growing to enjoy it. Not feeling crammed in a rat race of concrete and steel on a daily basis had done wonders for his writer's block. He couldn't help thinking that Amelia would love it here. If the court case went his way… He wouldn't allow himself to go there just yet. Turning, he saw Leigh staring at him. "What?"

Her cheeks turned a shade similar to her pale pink shirt. "Nothing…I just can't believe how different you look—clean-shaven."

They'd just left Klip and Dye on Main Street, where the salon's owner, a spirited, older woman named Alice, had cut his hair and shaved the days-old scruff off his chin. For the first time in weeks, he felt like his old self again. "Different good or different bad?"

Without answering, Leigh turned away and headed down a mall corridor.

Quickening his strides, Logan passed her; then walking backward in front of her, he said, "Admit it, you think I'm hot, don't you?"

Leigh scoffed, pushing him out of her way as she continued on.

He smiled. She *did.* She found him just as attractive as he found her. "Oh, come on, you must find me at least a little bit handsome…cute?…easy on the eyes?"

She paused and stared at him for a long moment. "You're…better looking in person than you are on your book covers," she said. "That's all you're getting. Fish for compliments somewhere else."

"I thought you said you hadn't seen my series." He hated those photos they insisted on putting on the book jackets. They always made him look stuffy and arrogant.

"I may have seen them somewhere in town."

He studied her. "Did you buy them?"

"I...may have," she said as she pulled him into the men's clothing store on their left.

"Hey, Leigh, what brings you by?" asked an older man hemming a pair of black dress pants behind the desk as they entered.

"Hi, Melvin. This guy needs your help... badly," she added with a smirk.

"What's the occasion?" Melvin asked, coming around the desk to size him up.

"The murder-mystery event at the community hall tomorrow night."

"Ah...Darlene Dawson strikes again," the man said with a nod. "I always hide in the stockroom whenever she comes in."

Leigh and Logan laughed.

"Hey, Melvin, do you have these pants in a thirty-six waist?" asked a man, coming out of the changing room holding a pair of dark charcoal dress pants. He was wearing only boxer briefs and gray dress socks.

At Logan's side, Leigh's eyes widened.

As she quickly turned away from the sight of the half-dressed man holding the pants, she collided with a rack of suit jackets, sending several to the floor.

"Shoot, sorry," she mumbled, bending to pick them up.

The man from the changing room also seemed surprised, but there was a trace of something else in his light blue eyes. Curiosity maybe? From their reactions to the sight of each other, Logan was guessing this was the infamous ex-husband. The jerk who'd left Leigh at her most vulnerable. He clenched his fists at his sides, and the hand in the cast spasmed in pain.

"I'm sorry, I didn't realize there was anyone else in the store," the ex said.

Of course. It was just a public mall, why would there be anyone else in the store? "Nice boxers," Logan said, ignoring the voice in his head telling him to be mature.

Glancing down at his pumpkin-orange boxers with the happy faces, the ex quickly covered himself with the pants he held, backing into the change room. "Thirty-sixes, Mel?" he said quickly before shutting the door.

"I'll take a look," Melvin said, heading toward the circular pants display. "I'll be with you folks in just a moment, once I get Neil straightened away."

"Take your time," Logan said. Turning to Leigh, who'd yet to regain her color from the sight of her ex in his boxer shorts, he said casually, "Someone you know?"

"There're not many people I don't know in Brookhollow," she said, avoiding his eyes. She headed for the far wall, where different-colored dress shirts hung on racks. Glancing at him quickly, she reached for a light gray one. "Size sixteen?"

"And a half," he said, folding his arms. "But I suspect you may know this particular man better than most?" He took the shirt she held out.

She continued to the tie tables, approaching the darker end of the spectrum of ties on display. "You're annoying."

"I've heard that before. So I'm right, that's him?"

Across the store, the man came out of the changing room again, this time fully dressed.

"Yes."

"Can I hit him?"

"No!"

Her loud exclamation caught the attention of the ex and the storekeeper.

"I guess she doesn't like this one," Logan said, quickly holding up a pink tie. Then dropping it, he whispered, "I mean normally I'm not that tough, but I'm sure this thing could pack a punch." He held up his cast.

Leigh laughed as she punched his arm. "Focus on ties," she said. Scanning them, she added, "I don't know you well enough to know what you might like."

"Don't you?" His hand covered hers as she reached for a black-and-silver-striped pattern.

The ex cleared his throat to their right. "Hi, Leigh."

They both turned to face him.

"Hi, Neil."

"Sorry about that."

Be sorry for interrupting.

"Don't be, it's…fine. Um, Neil, this is Logan Walters."

"Hey, man," Neil said, extending a hand.

Seriously? The last thing he wanted to do was shake this guy's hand. After the pain he'd caused Leigh. No way could he do it.

Leigh's elbow made contact with his side.

"Hi," he muttered, extending his left hand for a quick handshake, before letting Neil's drop as though he'd been burned.

"Well, I better go. See you. Pleasure meeting you, Logan," the ex said, but the jealousy and annoyance reflecting in his eyes were undeniable.

Good. Be jealous, be annoyed. It was about time Leigh was able to inflict the same kinds of emotions on her ex that she no doubt had to feel every time she saw him with his new family, which Logan suspected was often in the small town. He simply nodded as the ex walked away.

"Thank you for not making a scene," Leigh said.

"You're welcome," he said. "I only did it for you. I really could have taken him, you know."

CHAPTER EIGHT

THE NEW JERSEY Adoption Center in Newark was so quiet Leigh could hear the steady pounding of her heart in her chest as she waited in the front reception for Michelle Bennett the next morning. The dark tan clinic walls were covered with posters of happy, successful adoption stories and pictures of children with their adoptive and biological families—reminders that open adoption could be beneficial to all parties involved. On the coffee table in front of her were books of testimonials and letters of thanks to the clinic, but as she leafed through them, she found herself only growing more anxious. She wanted this so much, and to be this close…

The receptionist appeared in the waiting area, her file in hand. "Leigh, Michelle and Lise are ready for you. Would you like water or coffee?"

Leigh shook her head as she stood, wiping her sweaty palms in the legs of her dark gray dress pants. On shaky legs, she followed the receptionist down the hall to a room labeled Parent Meeting Room. She hesitated at the door, tugging at her cashmere sweater and tossing her hair over her shoulder. Why hadn't she worn something lighter? She felt as though she was suffocating in the thick blue turtleneck. She released a ragged breath as she reached for the door handle.

"Take your time. Go in when you're ready." The young woman smiled knowingly and handed her the file.

Leigh suspected she wasn't the first person to be paralyzed upon the realization that an adoption, quite possibly, was about to become a reality. "This happens a lot?"

"Every time," she said before leaving her alone in the hallway.

Leigh closed her eyes. She could do this. No matter what happened, she was prepared, she told herself. Taking several deep breaths, she turned the knob and entered the room quietly.

Michelle stood as she came in, but Leigh's gaze immediately went to the very pregnant young woman sitting on the love seat near the wall-mount fireplace. Inside the room were several chairs and even a small kitchenette. Michelle had said these meetings could take hours or minutes and be prepared for the first. "Hi, Leigh, come on in," she said now.

"Hi," the girl said with a nervous smile as she studied her. "Sorry, I'd get up but it's quite the process." She touched her large belly.

"No, no, don't worry."

"Is that your file?" Michelle asked.

"Oh yes." Leigh handed the file to Michelle with a shaky hand and scanned the room. The same comforting posters and encouraging quotes were on the walls.

"Thank you. Please sit, make yourself comfortable," the counselor said, laying the file on the table next to the other documents already in place.

Leigh sat across from Lise, unable to tear her eyes away. She couldn't be more than fifteen, and Leigh's heart went out to the girl in the sundress and sandals, a light Windbreaker draped across her lap. She knew from reading the information Michelle had left that Lise was a high-school student struggling to finish her diploma with the hopes of going to law school. The file had revealed that despite using protection, Lise had conceived the baby with her current boyfriend—a high-school senior whose parents were now forbidding him to have contact with her.

It angered Leigh that the boy's parents could be so narrow-minded as to think that Lise had gotten into this situation on her own. But Lise and her boyfriend had made the decision to not raise this baby so they could still have a chance at a future they wanted for themselves. To her, a decision like that took courage and she respected the girl across from her for her strength.

"Okay, where would you two like to start? Lise, would you like to ask Leigh your questions first?" Michelle asked, sitting in another armchair.

"Okay." She took a folded piece of paper

from her jacket pocket. "So, I just had a few..."

Leigh nodded. Waiting to take the bar exam couldn't be as hard as this.

"I know you live in a small town and own a day care. Do you plan on staying in Brookhollow permanently?"

"Yes, I do. Brookhollow has always been home. I have great friends and family there. I have no reason to move. As I explained to Michelle, my childhood consisted of a lot of traveling—my parents are missionaries—and, well, I would want my child...our child..." What was the correct term? "The baby to have more stability," she said.

"That's good. I like the idea of Ava growing up in a small town. Big cities scare me."

"Ava?" The baby was a girl? And her name was Ava? She couldn't help her surprise. She'd assumed that she would have the opportunity to name the baby...or at least be a part of the decision. Not being able to carry a baby to term, feel the life growing inside of her and being the first to hold the child after it was born was all hard enough…now this, too, had happened without her. She forced a breath. It didn't matter. What mattered was that in a few weeks she could have a baby girl.

"Yes, sorry, Leigh. I didn't mention it on the phone because it's at the discretion of the biological mother to reveal the sex of the child before the birth…as it sometimes affects the adoptive parents' decision." Michelle glanced between the two women.

"Did you want a girl?" Lise's face creased in worry as she asked.

A girl, a boy, it hadn't mattered, she'd just wanted a child of her own, but now hearing that this baby was a daughter, she realized how much she had been hoping for a little girl. "Yes, very much," she choked out.

The young woman's face lit up. "Do you want to see her?"

See her? The trembling of her hands that had temporarily subsided returned and she clasped them tightly on her lap. "You have an ultrasound picture?" Leigh's voice was barely more than a whisper and she wasn't sure how she'd managed any sound at all.

Lise retrieved the black-and-white image from her personal file on the table. “I leave it here in the file. It makes things a little easier than carrying it around with me,” she said sadly.

Tears brimmed in Leigh’s eyes, moved as she was by the girl’s courage. She couldn’t imagine how incredibly scared and nervous she must be going through this process. She was twice this teenager’s age and she was getting a baby, not giving one up, and she often found it hard to breathe whenever she thought about what they were doing.

“Here it is.” Lise extended the photo.

“Is it okay if I sit here?” she asked, moving to the love seat on Lise’s nod of approval. “Oh my…” She covered her mouth with her hand at the blurry yet distinct image of the baby —Ava—curled in a tiny ball. Her tiny hand was balled and her barely visible thumb was in her mouth.

“She’s beautiful,” Lise whispered, her eyes glued to the picture in Leigh’s hand.

“I couldn’t agree more,” Leigh said, staring at the image. This baby, this little girl, could be her child in a short few weeks. The room swam a little as she couldn't hold the tears back any longer. What if Lise decided she wasn't the right one to be a part of their lives? She felt as though she already was. Michelle had warned her, but nothing could have prepared her for the anxiety over the unknown.

Michelle leaned forward, and handed tissues to both women on the love seat, dabbing her eyes with one as well.

Composing herself, Leigh cleared her throat. "Sorry."

"Don't be, this is just the beginning of the tears, I assure you. This process is tough in the beginning, but it does get easier for everyone, I promise," Michelle added.

"Did you have other questions?" Leigh asked Lise, pulling her gaze from the photo momentarily.

"Yes, one. Um...the file says you're not married."

"I'm divorced. My ex-husband and I separated four years ago. We had tried for years to have a family of our own and when that wasn't possible, Neil ended the marriage," Leigh said.

"Do you think now that you might have a child, you two might get back together?" The hope in her eyes reminded Leigh so much of the hope she'd held on to for a long time after the divorce. Hope that had made it impossible to move on. Hope she'd learned to let go of.

"No. He's remarried now with two kids and another one on the way." She was surprised how the words weren't as hard to say as she would have thought.

"Oh." The girl was clearly disappointed. "I was kind of hoping the baby would have two parents."

The image of Logan flashed into her mind; she shook her head. Panic made her talk quickly. "That would be ideal, no doubt…but I can assure you, Ava would have the most loving adoptive parent and a wide circle of family and friends who would love her unconditionally." Leigh wasn't sure what else to say. And ultimately, there was nothing she could say to sway Lise's decision. The girl would make the choice she thought was right.

"Lise, would you like to show Leigh your birth-mother letter?" Michelle said.

Lise nodded.

"Birth-mother letter?" Leigh asked.

"Yes. Some mothers choose to write their feelings, their reasons for the adoption, their fears and hopes in a letter. It's often easier than saying the words out loud."

"Oh, okay," Leigh said as Lise handed her a piece of pink paper, torn on the ends and stained with small round circles. Teardrops.

Without even reading a word, Leigh felt her chest aching. This letter hadn't been easy for Lise to write, and she suspected it was going to take every ounce of her own strength to read it. "Can I take a minute?" she asked, feeling light-headed. In her excitement, she hadn't stopped to fully contemplate or understand how emotionally draining it would be.

"Of course," Michelle said. "Take all the time you need."

Lise reached across and placed a hand on Leigh's and the strength and comfort she found in the gesture gave her the courage to read.

Dear Baby Girl,
More than anything, please know that I love you. And that is why I want to give you this chance at a life I can't give you. Among my biggest fears is that you will think that I gave you up because I was a bad person, a selfish person. I know I have thought those things of myself. But the truth is, to prevent you from having the beautiful life you deserve would be selfish and wrong. I still feel like a child myself and in many ways I cannot care for you in the way you need. Through open adoption, I can be your friend and maybe someday someone you can respect and understand as having made this very difficult choice for you. I will watch you grow and develop into the incredible person you already are, and I will be proud that I was able to bring such a beautiful person into this world. I love you.
Love,
Your birth mom

The tears rolling down Leigh's face made it difficult to read the last line, but as she wiped her cheeks and handed back the letter, she quickly enveloped the young girl in a hug. She didn't move and neither did Lise as the tears fell.

THE CONNECTION WAS slower than usual. Or maybe she was just more impatient than usual. Either way she was desperate to see her parents on the screen, and it couldn't happen fast enough. The email she'd received from her mother earlier that day had said they were both available to chat that evening, and this time she was excited to share her news with them. The visit with the birth mother, Lise, had gone so well.

Her heart went out to the teenager and the tough choice she was making, and an unmistakable friendship had developed between them in that room.

The video chat screen opened and her parents' chins appeared. Leigh laughed. "Hey, guys! Nice chins."

"What?"

"Huh?"

"Move back from the screen." You

wouldn't know this wasn't their first time. Brilliant, successful medical professionals and they couldn't figure out a webcam to save their lives.

A second later, she could see them both. Or at least half of each of their faces—good enough.

"Hi, sweetheart, sorry I had to rush off last week," her dad said.

"It's okay, Dad. I'm glad you were free tonight, because I have some exciting news." Without pausing for a breath, she continued on, afraid the insecure connection would fail or her father's pager would once again delay the news. "It's a little premature…but…if everything goes well…you two are going to be grandparents." She paused and waited for the news to sink in.

The half of her mother's face she could see was blank. "You're pregnant?" she asked.

A natural assumption and one she should have expected, yet her mother's words still made her stomach knot. "No. I'm planning to adopt."

"Adopt?" Her father looked confused. "Like a baby?"

Leigh repressed the urge to roll her eyes. "No, Dad, a puppy. Yes, a baby." She hoped the exasperation in her voice wasn't as obvious over the computer.

"That's wonderful." Her mother finally produced the smile she'd been waiting for, but her polite tone was one she would have expected if she'd been revealing her news to an acquaintance. "When did you decide to do this?"

Leigh experienced a pang of guilt. *A long time ago.* "A little while ago."

"Those processes can take a long time, can't they?" Her father still sounded unsure.

"They can, but the agency has already placed my file on an upcoming adoption list. I met the mother of the child this morning. She's a teenager who plans to go to law school. She's smart and brave and wonderful...."

Her mother's smile faded. "You met her?"

Had they heard anything beyond that? "Yes. It will be an open adoption."

"I'm not sure what that means." Her father leaned closer until she could just see one penetrating eye behind his glasses.

"It means that the baby will always know that she was adopted. She'll have contact with her biological parents as well, if they want contact, but she'll be raised by..." Her. The realization was overwhelming. "Me," she said.

Her parents were silent.

She waited.

The silence continued.

"Say something!" This was amazing news she'd just shared with them. Sure, it was a lot to take in, but excitement was the appropriate response to this. Why couldn't her down-to-earth, practical parents just for once show the emotion she needed from them?

"This is great, sweetheart. Really, it is. Forgive us, it's just a surprise, that's all," her mother said.

"Yes, it is...and, as your mother said, it is great news," her father said slowly.

She felt a *but* coming on. "But?"

"No, no buts.... I just... Are you sure

you're done trying to have one on your own?" her father asked.

Her mother scowled at him. "Alan, don't be so insensitive."

"It's okay, Mom. Dad, each time I lost a baby, I lost a piece of myself." No one could possibly understand the pain of losing a child. Even one she'd never even held. "I'm turning thirty-nine in a couple of months and there are no men in sight." Except one who would be gone soon to piece together the home he couldn't lose. "This is what I want," she said without reservation.

"Well, then, sweetheart, I'm happy for you. Just be careful. I'd hate to see you disappointed again," he said.

"I will, Dad." She fought the deflation she felt. This was a great thing. This was what she wanted.

"Oh, and speaking of good news, we have some of our own," her mother said. Leigh couldn't help noticing that it seemed like an attempt to change the subject.

Those were her parents. She sighed and forced a smile. "What's up?"

"We're coming home next month."

Her eyes widened. "Really? I thought you were there until Christmas." This trip had been particularly long. They'd been stationed in South Africa for over a year, and only visited once.

"We are, but we decided to come home for Thanksgiving," she said.

Leigh smiled. "That's great. How long will you be home?"

"Just for Thanksgiving," her father said.

What did *just for Thanksgiving* mean? "You mean a weekend?"

"Just the day."

"*One day?* Are you serious? You're flying all the way from Africa for *one* day?" The travel time alone would take longer than their visit.

"Yes. I wouldn't, but your mom is homesick," her father said.

Leigh knew her father's priority in life had always been his missionary work. He accomplished such great change for the communities he visited, that his altruistic nature wasn't something anyone could criticize. But her mother hadn't known she was signing on for a lifetime of constant travel.

"Well, it'll be great to have you home, even if it is just a day," she said. Especially if she had her baby by then. She knew once her parents saw the child, they would forget their reservations.

"We should go now, honey, but we'll talk again soon." Her mother blew her a kiss through the screen and her father waved.

"Okay, love you, bye," she said as the connection closed.

She sat staring at the screen for a long moment, waffling between annoyance and disappointment. Really, what had she expected from them? She'd barely seen them in the past twenty-four years. They hadn't been in Brookhollow when she suffered through the miscarriages or the devastating divorce. For that matter, they hadn't even made it to her wedding. Her grandmother had walked her down the aisle and given her away. They might be her parents and she knew they loved her, but the support she needed would come, as it always did, from Grandma Norris.

Picking up her cell phone, she dialed the bakery, knowing that though it was after five, Ginger would still be there, preparing the dough for the morning. She rarely left the bakery before seven each night. At her age.

"We're closed. Call back in the morning," her grandmother said after the fourth ring. She sounded tired and more than a little grumpy—not her usual self.

"It's me, Grandma." No doubt her grandmother hadn't recognized her cell number on the call display. The older woman refused to own a cell phone or use one.

"Thank goodness. I've been taking orders for Thanksgiving pumpkin pies all day. I swear people start placing their orders earlier each year, and I don't understand why. It's not like I can bake them in advance. If I could, I would. Everything okay, darling?"

"Everything is great," she said, feeling some of her original excitement return. "I have wonderful news."

LOGAN WALKED INTO THE community hall the next evening and scanned the room for Leigh. She'd insisted on meeting him here, after much persuasion to even attend. Clearly, she didn't want this evening to be misconstrued as a date. *He* should be thinking as clearly as she was. After all, he was the one who couldn't move forward with her. In no uncertain terms. He'd only known her for less than three weeks. How could he trust his own response to her when he'd proven to be such a great judge of character with his ex-girlfriend?

Across the room, he spotted her. He blinked. At least he thought it was her. She wore a floor-length black dress with a deep slit in the side, and her dark hair curled around her shoulders. He had to move closer, squinting in the dim lighting, to be sure she was the same woman who'd helped him figure out a new series ending.

She turned as he approached, and she smiled, clearly relieved to see him. "Hi."

"You look amazing." He leaned in and kissed her cheek, feeling her stiffen as her gaze swept the room around them.

She tugged at the tight fabric along her hips. "I haven't worn this dress in a million years.... I can't believe you talked me into coming."

"It's not the dress, it's you, and stop

fussing with it." Draping an arm around her waist, he said, "I still don't understand how you live in this town with the people you grew up with and see every day, and yet you feel uncomfortable at events like this." While he'd initially been opposed to the idea of playing such an integral role in that evening's events, he had to admit he was looking forward to it now.

"I'm just more of a homebody, I guess," she said.

"Is that the story you're sticking to or will I get the real answer if I pry a little more?" he asked, leading the way to the bar in the corner of the room.

"I'm sticking."

He'd see about that. "Fine. What are you drinking?"

"Oh, just a diet..." She started in mid-scan around the room, and abruptly turned. "A martini, two olives," she told the bartender.

Logan turned to look at what she'd seen. The ex stood talking to a group several feet away. His arm was draped around the waist of a woman who Logan would guess was five months pregnant, maybe six.

Neil and his new wife: the real reason she avoided these events. He didn't need any more explanation than the expression on her face.

"Sticking, huh?" he whispered, before handing her the drink and ordering his own. "A beer please." He laid several bills on the bar and left the change.

"Which table are we sitting at?" She accepted her martini and took a gulp.

"Not that one," Logan said, nodding toward the table where her ex-husband stood. Taking his beer, and placing a hand on her back—bare in the open dress, he realized—he led her to the other side of the room. Holding his breath, he checked their tickets for their assigned table number. Fourteen. Far away from the ex and his new wife.

"There you are," came Darlene Dawson's unmistakable voice from behind them.

Turning, he smiled.

"Hi, Leigh, it's great to see you. I have to say, I was shocked when Mr. Walters here called to ask for the additional ticket. We can never get you out to these events.

You look beautiful," she said, more than a hint of curiosity in her bright blue eyes.

"Thank you. The center looks wonderful, Darlene. You sure know how to organize an event." Leigh sipped her martini.

"I'm pleased with it," she said. "And Mr. Walters saved the day by agreeing to participate." She lowered her voice. "So, Logan, here is your guidebook. All your lines and tasks are outlined."

Logan quickly tucked it into his jacket pocket.

"Thanks again! You really are a dear for volunteering to help," Darlene said as she dashed off.

"I'm not sure volunteering would be the word I would use," Logan muttered as he pulled out a chair for Leigh.

"Thanks," she said as she sat.

"Leigh!"

"Oh no," she groaned as Logan turned in his seat.

The pregnant redhead was approaching, her baby bump the only indication that she was expecting, as she glided gracefully across the room in silver three-inch heels.

Leigh's smile looked forced. "Angela, hi."

"Hi, yourself. Wow, I'm shocked to see you here," Angela said, but her eyes were on Logan.

"Angela, this is Logan."

He extended a hand.

"Nice to meet you," she said, looking from him to Leigh. "So, Leigh, you haven't gotten back to me about available space and I hate to be pushy but I have to make a decision soon about where to send the kids if you aren't able to take them."

Leigh hesitated. "Oh, well, as I said last week, I'm still not sure…."

Available space? At the day care? The woman couldn't possibly be serious. She expected Leigh to take care of her ex-husband's children? Children she hadn't been able to give him?

"Please let me know as soon as space opens." She patted her belly and laughed. "Three spaces actually."

Leigh's face contorted in a painful effort at a smile, and Logan squeezed her hand under the table. The nerve of this woman was too much.

"I'll be sure to let you know as soon as anything opens up," Leigh choked out.

"Great, thanks. Enjoy your evening. I can't wait to find out who the murderer is."

As she walked away, Logan turned to Leigh. "Do I get to choose who I kill?"

Reaching into his jacket pocket, he scanned the game play booklet Darlene had given him.

Leigh placed a hand over his, covering the book. "She's not a bad person." She drained the contents of her martini glass and reached for the glass of champagne on the table.

"I don't care how many spaces become available, you cannot agree to watch those kids. I can't believe they would even ask."

"I run the only day care in town."

Logan tilted her face up to look into her dark eyes. "You do not need to watch those kids."

"Welcome, everyone!" Darlene's voice at the podium made it impossible to say anything else. "Thank you all for coming out. Tonight we have a fun-filled murder-mystery event, the first one we've ever tried at the community hall, and I think it will be a great success. I'll remind participants to consult their booklets for how to proceed throughout the evening. Enjoy the dinner and I hope we all make it out alive," she said.

At the chorus of applause, waiters appeared from the corner of the darkened room with the salads.

"Logan!" a woman said from the next table.

Logan recognized the waitress from the café on Main Street. He hadn't been back to Joey's since the day he'd met her.

He couldn't remember her name and he searched his memory for the image of her name tag. "Hi..."

"April," she said.

"Right, from the diner, I remember. Sorry, I'm not great with names."

"No worries. I've been hoping you'd stop into Joey's before you left town, and I've been meaning to stop by the B-and-B to thank you."

Thank him? He couldn't remember helping her with anything. "For?" Logan asked.

"For cluing me in to my boyfriend's romantic streak, which got me to go on that haunted hike. Jonathan proposed," she said with a wide smile, extending her left hand in their direction.

The single solitaire sparkled in the low light of the candles on the tables. "Wow, congratulations, April, that's great," Leigh said.

"Yes, congrats. Glad I'm so good at spotting romance a mile away," Logan said, looking pointedly at Leigh, who just sat there staring at him.

Across the table, Danielle O'Connor from Dog Eared Books waved, catching their attention. "I thought that was you, but without the beard, I wasn't sure," she said, leaning forward, past the large centerpiece of black and white roses.

His clean-cut look *was* quite the transformation. He hadn't even remembered what he looked like without the beard. Klip and Dye on Main Street had done wonders cleaning him up, and Leigh's appreciative assessment the evening before had revealed she approved of the new clean-shaven appearance. "Have you changed your mind about the desk yet?"

"Desk?" Leigh glanced between him and the bookstore owner.

"The Cutler rolltop in my store," Danielle explained. "He thinks he can get his hands on it, but he's out of his league!"

"Oh," Leigh said. "Wow, have you met everyone in town?"

"Almost." Logan winked.

Across the table Danielle laughed as she opened her purse and reached inside. "I did find one for sale in Boston. Some family-estate sale—it was posted two days ago. . . ." She handed the listing across the table to him.

Logan studied the picture. "She's beautiful," he said. "Enduring."

"I wouldn't imagine she'll last long. I'd call about it right away if you're interested," Danielle said.

"I will, thank you." He appreciated her thoughtfulness, but with the possibility of a move, buying the desk didn't seem likely.

"My pleasure. I wanted a way to repay you for your help with those grant-application forms. It turns out we may qualify for one after all. Fingers crossed."

Leigh looked at him. "Grant applications?"

"Yeah, I just mentioned that there may

be some government funding available seeing as the store is housed in a government building and it's been in business so long." Taking a sip of his beer, he leaned back in his chair.

"Wow." Leigh's expression was one of disbelief and—dare he hope?—admiration?

"What?"

"You've been busy, that's all," she said.

"I've had some free time," he said with a shrug, resting his cast on the back of her chair.

"So, what else have you been doing during your time here?"

"Mostly I've just been falling in love..." He watched her swallow hard. "With this town...and the people in it."

LOGAN'S DISAPPEARANCE from the table was so brief that only Leigh noticed, and while he was gone her mind reeled. Falling in love with the town and the people in it... Her heart had all but stopped as he'd said it, and now she couldn't force the words from her mind. What exactly had he meant? Was he falling in love with her, as well? Did that mean that no matter what happened in court, he could take a chance on creating a new home with her?

A week from now that court could decide that his daughter would live permanently with her mother in California and he'd be moving there, as well. Would she consider moving with him? But…the open adoption.

Then again, what if the case went his way?

She didn't have time to ponder the idea as he took his seat next to her again and the lights in the community hall immediately went out. Gasps and a loud scream could be heard echoing on the walls of the center, before the lights flickered back on. Immediately, three actors dressed as policemen were stationed at each of the entrances to the community center. Leigh shot a quick glance at Logan, and the wide grin he wore spoke volumes.

She opened her mouth to speak, but he placed a finger on her lips.

"Shh."

Darlene Dawson appeared once more at the microphone, suitably panicked. An older man in a trench coat followed behind her across the stage. "Sorry for the interruption, everyone, but there seems to have been a murder."

The crowd uttered the appropriate shock and horror and Leigh eagerly awaited what would happen next. Though she knew the murderer was Logan, she was intrigued to see how this would play out.

This was turning out much better than she could have anticipated and she was having fun. The handsome man beside her had a lot to do with it. More than she wanted to admit. Falling in love with the town and the people? She stole a glance toward him.

The short man in the trench coat took the microphone, adjusting it to his height. "Hello, everyone. I'm Detective Adams and I regret to inform you there is a murderer in your midst." He paused, checking the folded piece of paper he held in his hand. "As you may have noticed, we have assigned police officers to all doors and no one will be permitted to enter or exit until the murderer is in custody. As of right now, everyone is a suspect and will not be permitted to leave the room without an escort. Not even to go to the washroom."

A murmur ran through the crowd. From the table across the room, Neil stood. "I can't find my wife," he said in concern.

Leigh whipped her head around to face Logan, her eyes wide. "You didn't," she whispered.

Suppressing a smile, he avoided her gaze as he shrugged.

Oh, he did. She laughed. The temptation to kiss him was overwhelming. Of course she'd never wish Neil or Angela or their family any real harm, but in this fake, safe situation, she couldn't help feeling intense satisfaction.

"I'm sorry to inform you, Mr. Conway, but it was your wife who was murdered this evening," the detective confirmed.

CHAPTER NINE

LEIGH INHALED, BREATHING in the sweet aroma of cheesecake and cinnamon buns escaping through the front door of her grandmother's bakery. She shuffled her feet through the crunchy leaves on the wide, brick-patterned sidewalk on Main Street far too early the next morning. The late night the evening before hadn't been a great idea, but despite her tired eyes and the slight throbbing in her brain, she couldn't bring herself to regret it. However, the kids would be arriving in less than an hour and she'd neglected to prep the day before. The front door of Ginger Snaps was locked, but she could see her grandmother behind the counter, placing the pastry trays in the showcase. Seventy-four, and the only day she didn't work was Monday when she visited her friends at the seniors' complex. She knocked once and waved.

Ginger unlocked the dead bolt. "Come on in, honey," she said, ushering her inside.

Leigh locked the dead bolt behind her and followed her grandmother into the kitchen. "Need some help?" She had to hurry, but she hated that her grandmother always worked this early shift alone. She *was* seventy-four, after all.

"I've got it all under control." Ginger Norris set the tray aside and hugged her. When she pulled away, flour covered the front of Leigh's purple sweatshirt. "Oh dear, look at the mess of you," she said, grabbing a dish towel and fanning at it.

"It's okay, don't worry." She'd pulled on her yoga pants and an old Brookhollow High sweatshirt that was a million years old. Certainly not the evening gown she'd been wearing less than eight hours ago. She yawned.

"Tired?"

"I'm barely awake," she said, helping her grandmother move the croissants from the cookie sheet to the Plexiglas display case.

"Late night?" Her grandmother's tone was a little bit know-it-all.

It was only seven o'clock in the morning; how had her grandmother heard about her evening already? "Yes, I went to the murder-mystery party at the community hall—as if you don't already know." Leigh rested her hip against the counter.

"You usually skip those things."

"Yeah…well…Logan Walters—the guest at the bed-and-breakfast I told you about—well, he was cornered by Darlene Dawson a few days ago, and he didn't want to go alone." She toyed with the fringed end of the sweatshirt.

"This is the man you're helping with his book?" Her grandmother continued to work, but Leigh knew she had the woman's full attention.

"Yes." She hadn't told anyone about her helping Logan except her grandmother, and at the time it hadn't seemed like a big deal. Today it did.

"I thought he would be gone by now."

Any day now. "Not yet."

"Soon?" The hopeful note in her grandmother's voice caught her attention.

"The book is almost finished and his hand is healing nicely, so yes, soon." Her attempt to hide her disappointment failed and she quickly changed the subject. "Anyway, I didn't get my usual baking done last night, so I'm going to need a box of gingerbread cookies."

Her grandmother stopped working and turned to face her. "Be careful, Leigh. You have big plans. Can he really fit into them? Please don't give up on your dream of adopting for the possibility of a shot with this man you've only known for a couple of weeks." The older woman's warning was gentle but firm.

She didn't need reminding. She was closer than ever to having a baby, and she wasn't losing sight of that. "I know, Grams. Don't worry, I haven't forgotten," she said. "Besides, it's not what everyone thinks—I'm just helping him write his book."

A week ago that had been true. Now she wasn't convinced. Especially when her chest tightened at the thought of typing *The End* on his manuscript.

"Sweet girl, I've seen that look before… on your mother's face…when she tried to convince me your dad was just her boss. They were just assigned together, she'd say. Yeah, right. They were in love before that first plane landed. I knew better then and I suspect I'm right again now."

Leigh lowered her gaze. There would be no fooling her grandmother about her growing feelings for the man.

Ginger lifted her chin. "I don't want to see you get hurt. Lord knows you've had your share of heartache."

"Believe me, Grandma, it's nothing," she lied, desperate to push aside her feelings for Logan. For the sake of the open adoption process, she couldn't even entertain the thought of involving someone else at this stage, for fear of ruining the progress she'd made.

"Well, for the sake of your future, it should stay that way," her grandmother warned. "Be patient, Leigh. The right man is out there. Logan Walters is not him."

MAIN STREET WAS quiet and still in the early morning. Exactly what Logan's conflicted mind needed. Despite the late night and the even later session of staring at the ceiling that had followed, he was wide-awake. A cool breeze rustled the leaves at his feet as he continued to walk, with no direction or purpose except to calm the frazzled thoughts plaguing him. A chapter away from the end of his series, surprisingly a week before the deadline he'd been certain he'd never make, and he wasn't feeling the relief he'd expected. Finishing the book meant leaving Brookhollow, leaving Leigh. Beautiful, caring, amazing Leigh. A woman he shouldn't feel so connected to after only two and a half weeks of knowing her, yet the chemistry between them was unmistakable.

He might have been oblivious of the romance developing on the pages of his manuscript, but there was no denying it in his own life. A romance that hinged on the success of his court hearing in two weeks time.

He couldn't ask her to give up her life here to follow him, to take a chance on a relationship that might possibly be what they'd both been missing. Could he? And could he really trust what he was feeling?

At one time, he'd also believed in his feelings for Kendra.

Scanning the storefronts, Logan spotted Ginger Snaps, her grandmother's bakery. Despite his confusing, conflicting thoughts, a warm smile spread across his face as he remembered the night before. He warmed at the thought of Leigh. He'd never before met anyone quite like the beautiful brunette with the big brown eyes and gentle laugh. Her troubled past only seemed to magnify her kindness and her ability to maintain a positive outlook on life.

A bell jingled as he pushed open the door to the bakery a moment later, guided by the smell of cinnamon rolls and coffee. His stomach growled. Thankfully the muffins were healthy; he suspected he'd be consuming more than one that morning. And caffeine was a necessity.

An older woman glanced up from behind the till, and a frown clouded her youthful eyes. Leigh's grandmother. She could be Leigh years from now. The same deep brown eyes, slightly upturned nose and soft, round cheeks as her granddaughter, the woman had aged beautifully. Good genes clearly ran in the Norris family. He found himself wondering if Leigh's mother bore the same striking resemblance. He could imagine a stunning family photo. Meeting the women's stern expression, he sobered and straightened. Clearing his throat, he approached the counter. "Good morning."

Ginger looked at the clock on the wall. "We don't open until eight."

Logan glanced at his watch: 7:56. "Sorry, the door was open and the open sign was lit up. I'm Logan Walters. I'm staying at—"

"I know who you are," the older woman said curtly. She took a stack of bills from the register and slid them into a bank deposit bag.

Tough lady. He suspected rumors were circulating around town about the time he was spending with Leigh. Rumors the older woman wasn't keen on.

A young girl approached from the back. "Ginger, I'll take that over to the bank for you before we open," she said.

"That's okay, I got it." She pushed

through the swinging gate to join Logan on the other side of the counter. "Walk with me," she said, jerking her head toward the door.

Logan's mouth dropped and he pointed to his chest. "Me?"

"Yes."

"Um...I just came in for coffee. Leigh also mentioned raspberry muffins..." he stammered. The small-town hospitality didn't appear to extend inside Ginger Snaps. He suspected this Ginger could indeed snap. Apparently the similarities between generations ended on the outside.

"We're out."

"I just took a batch from the oven," the girl behind the counter told Ginger in puzzlement.

"Those are for Leigh," the shop owner interrupted, shooting Logan a sideways glance. She opened the front door and stepped outside, holding the door for him.

Sighing, Logan followed. So much for breakfast. He should have gone to Joey's. They liked him there.

Outside, keeping up with the short woman's quick strides proved surprisingly challenging. "Am I in trouble, Mrs. Norris?" he asked with a nervous laugh when she didn't speak immediately.

Ginger paused, studying him. "Not yet, but I suspect you will be—left to your own devices." She continued walking.

"I'm not sure I understand."

"For falling in love with my granddaughter," she said bluntly.

Logan stumbled over a crack in the sidewalk and fought to catch his balance. The accident-causing gene seemed to run in the family, as well, he thought. The Norris women were dangerous. And falling in love? Was Leigh falling in love? "I don't think you understand my interest in Leigh." That didn't sound right. Probably because it was a lie. "I mean, my involvement." That wasn't much better. *Come on, you're a bestselling author. Words shouldn't be this difficult.* Words, no. *Lies,* yes. "Leigh is just helping me," he said simply, holding up his cast. "I can't do much with this." That was true at least.

An image of her in the formfitting black evening gown the night before made his palms sweat.

They stopped in front of the bank. “Wait here,” she instructed, disappearing inside.

Logan sighed, watching her approach the tellers with her deposit. *Wait here.* The temptation to sprint in the opposite direction was overshadowed with the desire to set things right for Leigh’s sake. He raked his good hand through his hair as he watched Ginger complete her transaction and come out of the bank. She nodded in the direction of the bakery and began walking, but didn’t speak.

Was he supposed to say something? “Look, I know that we’ve been spending time together besides working—the party last night and the haunted hike last week…” Logan fell into step beside her.

“The haunted hike?”

“You hadn’t heard that one?” he asked.

“No.”

“Shoot.”

She picked up angry speed and Logan jogged a few paces ahead, then stopped in front of her.

“Please, just hear me out.” Never before had he felt the need to explain himself to a stranger, but somehow he felt he owed it to Leigh.

Ginger folded her arms and tapped her foot impatiently.

"You're from here. You must know how rumors can spread, whether they're accurate or not." Logan raised an eyebrow.

"But you just admitted to taking my granddaughter to the Monroes' haunted hike."

"Yes, I did, but it was just for research."

She took a step toward him and said sadly, "Maybe for you. Look, a half-hearted failed attempt is worse than no attempt at all…and if it's true that you're not in love with my granddaughter, then maybe you should do your research alone. Leigh can't trust someone just passing through."

Logan remained silent, suddenly unsure if lying about his growing feelings for Leigh only compounded the wrongs. Now the woman thought he was simply using her granddaughter, which was worse.

At the doorway, Ginger stopped and searched his face. "Come in, I'll get you those muffins. I suspect, despite my warnings, you'll see Leigh before I do."

"LOGAN?" THE BLONDE nurse at the medical clinic stood in the waiting room with his file an hour later.

He'd arrived early for his checkup with the doctor who'd set his cast a few weeks before and he glanced up from the *Men's Health Magazine* he was reading. "Yeah?" he said through a mouthful of raspberry muffin.

"I can take you in now," she said.

Logan shoved the rest into his mouth and turned to look at the big, muscular guy sitting in the chair next to him. In his loose-fitting track pants and UFC T-shirt that barely fit around his expanding biceps, the guy had probably already read that month's issue of *Men's Health*—several times. "He was here first."

Logan hadn't made an appointment, as he didn't think the medical clinic would be busy that time of day.

The nurse folded her arms across her chest as she shot the other man a wary look. "I'm making him wait. Your injury was from helping someone. This guy's was from pure stupidity."

The young man just laughed and nodded.

Obviously some personal history there. Setting the magazine aside, Logan stood. "Sorry, man," he said.

"Don't sweat it, buddy. I'm used to it."

Logan followed the nurse down the hall. "Friend of yours?" he asked.

The nurse whose name tag read Lindsay scoffed. "Are you kidding me? No." She opened the door to an exam room and ushered him inside. "That guy is trouble and that's all he'll ever be. He trains MMA at Extreme Athletics here in town and he's in here every other week with an injury."

"Not a fan of MMA?"

"Not a fan of self-inflicted injuries from overtraining or allowing yourself to be brutally beaten and passing it off as an athletic sport."

He couldn't say he disagreed with the brutality of the sport. The last pay-per-view he'd seen, the fighter had broken his leg in two different places. It certainly wasn't his thing. "He looks pretty tough, though."

"Ha. They all act tough, but if you've ever seen them slide into the confined, tight space of an MRI machine, you'd know better."

She took his blood pressure and examined the cast.

"Dr. Harris will be in shortly to check your cast. Don't get your hopes up, though. Adult bones don't heal as quickly as children, so I would say you have another few weeks of wearing this yet."

Normally the realization that his hand had to remain in a cast would be cause for annoyance, but today he found himself relieved. He didn't need or want an excuse not to employ Leigh's help to finish this book. The night before he'd been close to telling her how he felt about her. The only thing holding him back had been the uncertainty of her feelings for him or what they would do about it. He had decided to wait…until there was more clarity or indication from her of her own feelings. "That's fine."

Lindsay smiled. "I bet it is."

"READY FOR THE last chapter?" Leigh asked, her hands poised over the keys of his laptop that evening.

Not at all. "Almost, but first, your grandmother gave me these to give to you." Logan laid the bag of muffins on the table. "There's a couple missing, I'm not sure what happened," he said, desperate to keep what could potentially be their last evening together light, her grandmother's warning echoing in his ears. The woman was mean, but she was right. Leigh deserved better than another failed attempt at a relationship.

Leigh whipped around to face him. "Grandma Norris? You saw her?"

Logan nodded, jamming his hands in his jean pockets. "We, uh, had a chat."

Leigh groaned before pulling out a muffin. "What did she say? Did she yell at you?" She shook her head as she bit into the muffin.

"Don't worry, it was nothing. She was just concerned about you." He paused. "I assured her there was nothing to worry about. That there was nothing going on between us."

She didn't disagree. "Right, of course there isn't. I'm just helping you finish your book, that's all. Thank you for setting her straight."

He cleared his throat as he said, "You look at lot like her."

Leigh gave a small laugh. "I know. It's a little odd knowing exactly what I'll look like at seventy-four."

"Still beautiful."

They stared at each other for a long moment.

Leigh was the first to break eye contact. "Okay," she said, "let's get started."

LEIGH FOUGHT TO keep her focus on the screen as she typed the words Logan dictated. He thought she was beautiful…yet he'd told her grandmother there was nothing going on between them. Then again, so had she. She'd been lying. Had he been lying, as well? With each word closer to the end, she prayed the computer would crash.

"A gunshot split the air…."

She stopped typing.

"Gunshot?" All other thoughts forgotten, she stared wide-eyed at him. "I thought you were changing the ending."

Logan smiled. "Keep typing."

Leigh typed the words and waited.

"The force of Piper's body crashing into him as they fell to the warehouse floor…"

Leigh typed furiously. Piper took the bullet? Wait a minute…Logan wasn't planning to kill her off instead? That defeated the whole purpose of not killing Van. Had he even been listening at all? "Logan…"

"Shh—type."

Ten minutes later, Leigh released a sigh of relief as she let the blinking cursor linger at the end of the final paragraph. "She saved his life."

"Yes. And then they lived happily ever after." Logan sat on the bench next to her.

"Want to do the honors?" she asked, sliding the laptop toward him. She could only imagine how finishing this book must feel. Besides, there was no way she could be the one to end things.

"Not right now," he said, turning to face her. "You know, I never actually typed the end on any of the other books. It always felt too definite, too final…and I knew there was more to come." His gaze met hers and he touched her hand.

"But this is the end," she whispered.

"It doesn't have to be," he said, and she knew they were no longer talking about the book.

She swallowed hard. "Logan—"

"Just hear me out before you say anything. Moving from one foster home to another as a kid and then running away, well, *home* is a powerful word for me. I thought I had finally found my home with Kendra, and look how that turned out. But here, it's different—"

"Brookhollow does have that feeling of home," she said.

"You're interrupting," he chided, touching her cheek. "It's not Brookhollow, Leigh, it's you."

"Logan, I—"

"You really don't know how to not speak, do you? Maybe this will work," he said, closing the gap between them and kissing her. His lips were soft as they met hers.

Shocked, Leigh sat frozen, arms at her sides, unable—though not unwilling—to return the kiss. What was he doing? She was only weeks from adopting a child, something he didn't know anything about.

She couldn't deny that she had feelings for Logan, and only her sensibility prevented her from wrapping her arms around his neck and returning the kiss that moment and every moment from then on.

Logan tensed as he moved away, his eyes searching her face. "Leigh."

Just the sound of her name on his lips, his voice drenched in unconcealed emotion, was enough to make her want to alter all of her plans and take a chance on a relationship with him. Move to L.A. if that's where he took her.

But an image of the ultrasound of the baby—Ava—brought her back to reality.

Removing his hands from her face, she stood, struggling to force a deep breath. Turning her back to him, she failed to find the words to explain. Words she should have said a long time ago.

He was the one to break the silence. "I'm sorry, I guess I'm not as good at reading people as I thought."

Behind her she could hear him shut the

laptop with a snap, and unzip the case. She couldn't let him leave without saying something…telling him he was right to have kissed her—only not really, because this connection between them couldn't go anywhere for more reasons than just his.

Turning back, she said, "No, you read the situation perfectly and I'm sorry I let my feelings for you show."

The man of her dreams had kissed her only seconds before, and there wasn't a thing she could do but let him go.

"I'm not…" Logan paused but kept his distance. "Leigh, if you're worried about me, don't be. I'm a writer. I can live anywhere…and as I was trying to explain, Brookhollow is only the second place I've ever found that I hadn't wanted to escape. Here, life is so different. You are different."

He was making this hard. The worst part was that he was right—he could stay… if everything went well with the custody hearing.

Still unsure how to tell him about the adoption, she stalled, "What about Amelia? You said yourself, if the judge awards

Kendra full custody, you'll be on the first plane to California." He had said as much. She'd almost felt better knowing that they'd both had reasons why this couldn't work. Now he was acting as though there was nothing standing in their way of a relationship.

He moved toward her then, a sad longing in his dark eyes, illuminated only by the gazebo lights. "That's really a question for you. I was hoping that if you feel even half as much about me as I've come to feel for you over these last three weeks, then if I have to go, you would come with me. I mean, not right away, of course…but we could see how things progressed, and then eventually…"

There it was—the sacrifice. One so much bigger than he could imagine he was asking her to make. If she wanted to be with him, there was the chance that she would have to give up her home, her business, Brookhollow, and in a few short weeks, it wouldn't be just her life a decision like that would impact.

It was a sacrifice she wasn't willing to make. Couldn't make if she went ahead with the open adoption—it wouldn't be fair to Ava or Lise. For the first time in her life, she was about to get the family she'd been waiting for.

"Brookhollow is home for me, Logan."

"You won't even consider this? Won't even consider us? Look, I know what I'm asking is huge. Asking you to give up everything if that's what the court decides. But think about what you'd be gaining—a family, me, a stepdaughter. And we don't even know if it's even necessary yet. Things might go my way."

The desperate hope in his voice brought tears to her eyes. She would have moved in a heartbeat a year ago, if he'd asked; she would have. But now, despite her growing love for this man, she refused to abandon everything she'd worked hard to achieve.

"Wow, I really did read us wrong," Logan said, in a voice devoid of emotion.

He packed up his notebooks, throwing them into the case and zipping it quickly. He tossed it over his shoulder and bounded down the stairs of the gazebo.

Leigh watched him go, fighting every instinct to stop him. This was the way this was always supposed to go. He was always leaving. She was always letting him.

"No, I refuse to accept this," he said, and turned to face her.

His confusion and hurt were too much, and she lowered herself down to the bench, not trusting her knees.

"You can't honestly be letting me walk away like this. We can figure this out," he said in exasperation.

"I'm adopting a baby, Logan." There, she'd said it. The words were out. At least she thought she'd said them out loud. When she raised her gaze to his, there was no doubt that he'd heard them.

"You're adopting a child?"

"Yes."

"Since when?"

"Since before we met."

"I'm… What… Why?" He shook his head and, dropping his laptop case to the grass, he looked off into the distance. "Why didn't you say anything?"

"I didn't tell anyone, other than Grandma and Rachel."

"I'd like to think I'm not just anyone."

"You were at one time." She hadn't

meant the words to pack such a punch, but he reeled from the impact. "I'm sorry, I meant when we first met."

"That day seems like a lifetime ago. So much has changed in a couple of weeks. We shared things, Leigh."

"This was one thing I couldn't share."

"Even though you could tell that I was starting to fall for you? Forget that, what about the fact that you can deny it all day long, but I know you're falling in love with me, too. Didn't that make things different? Didn't that put me on the list of people who should know what your plans were?"

"I never expected…this."

"Never expected what, Leigh?" he demanded, taking long strides toward her.

She shifted on the bench and averted her gaze. This was a nightmare. Why couldn't he just walk away? Leave?

He crouched in front of her, forcing her to meet his eyes. "Never expected what, Leigh?" he repeated.

"I never expected to fall in love with you. It doesn't make a difference, though, does it?" She jumped up and moved away from him. "I'm adopting a child, Logan, in a few weeks. I've met with the birth mother. I've seen the ultrasound. I love this child already and it's everything I've always wanted, so me loving you changes nothing. You have your daughter to think about and I'm getting the family I've always dreamed of."

"Really? The family you've always dreamed of seems to be missing a piece."

She stiffened.

"Have you even considered how hard it will be to raise a child on your own?"

She swung around, her eyes blazing. "How dare you? Of course I have—every day for the last four years, in fact. I can't have a child of my own and it turns out that no men around here want a woman who can't give them a house full of kids."

"Neil was not every man," Logan said.

"What do you know about it, anyway, Logan?" Tears threatened to fall and she was desperate to get away from him.

"I know what it's like to grow up not knowing where you came from. Leigh, this child will wonder…"

She swallowed hard.

"This is going to be hard, and doing it alone will make it that much harder."

She somehow found the strength to say, "I can do it," proud that her voice remained steady, despite her churning anxiety.

"Okay, maybe you're okay with doing this alone, but what about this child? Don't you think he or she deserves a father?"

Her shoulders shook and the tears she'd been successful in holding back gave way, trailing down her cold cheeks. That nagging thought had been the one thing over the years preventing her from going ahead with adoption before now. The uneasy feeling that maybe she would be cheating a child out of a home with two parents—a mother and a father.

Common sense had convinced her that families came in all shapes and sizes, and if you waited for the ideal situation, you would be waiting a long time. But now hearing the words from Logan brought back all her self-doubt. She wouldn't allow him to do that to her. Clearly, she didn't know him as well as either of them believed. "You can go now."

"Leigh—"

"No, Logan. Nothing you can say will change this ending."

"WHAT CAN I GET YOU?" a distracted female bartender asked fifteen minutes later, placing a square paper napkin in front of Logan on the bar. Her tone was curt, short, not quite unfriendly, but definitely preoccupied.

That was fine with him. The last thing he wanted right now was to entertain small talk with anyone. That evening should have gone a whole lot differently. He should be celebrating the end of the book, the end of the series and the beginning of something with Leigh. Instead he was sitting alone in the town's hot spot.

The pool-hall portion where he sat appeared to be the club section of the room, as he noticed a few girls dancing on a ten-by-ten tiled dance floor near the pool tables in the corner. Through a set of glass doors to his right, he could see a bowling alley, currently flashing neon lights for glow bowling and a sign near the washrooms indicated the movie theater was just at the end of the hall. “Just a soda.”

“If that’s all you want, there’s a convenience store about two blocks east.” The woman pointed to the left, one hand on her hip.

Logan almost smiled. Aah, finally some attitude, finally a bit of realism in this twilight zone of a place. Finally an attitude that mirrored his own that evening. “Yes, well, I’m very much enjoying the pleasant atmosphere in here, so if it’s all the same to you, I’d rather have a watered-down, overpriced soda from the bar.”

The woman’s face broke into a wide grin and she shook her head as she reached for a tall glass and poured the drink. She set the drink down on the mahogany bar. “On the house.”

“Why?”

“Because that’s my first smile all day. I’m Melody.”

“Logan—”

“Walters, I know,” Melody said with a nod.

“Does everyone know?”

“Let’s see, you’ve been in town almost three weeks…so yeah…everyone in Brookhollow knows…and probably everyone in Brook Haven, the next town over." Melody turned her attention to the drink order slip the waitress from the bowling alley placed on the bar. She poured several beers from the tap and set them on a tray, sliding it toward the girl. At the till, she punched in the drink order before turning her attention to a textbook on the counter in front of her.

"Studying?" A moment ago, he hadn't been in any mood to talk.

"Attempting to."

"Must be difficult with all the noise and distractions in here," he said, taking a sip of the soda.

"Believe it or not, I get more done here than at home." She nodded to the pictures of twin boys posted to the mirror behind the shelves stacked with liquor bottles.

He would guess the boys were seven, maybe eight—around the same age as Amelia. He recognized them as two of the kids Leigh had taken to the pumpkin patch. "Children can be the biggest distraction of all."

"I've heard that staying at the bed-and-breakfast can get a bit loud sometimes."

"It can, but it's a good loud…though I didn't always think that way." When he first arrived the sound had nearly broken his heart and in the midst of his writer's block, the sound had been torturous.

"I heard that, too."

Logan cocked his head to the side. "What else have you heard?"

"That you broke your wrist trying to help Leigh, so in turn she helped you with your book…and that you two have created quite a stir with your appearances around town, including a run-in with Neil and a pair of orange boxer shorts with… Wait a second…what was it on his shorts?" She tapped the bar.

"Happy faces," he said.

"Happy faces, that's it!"

"Well, it seems like the rumor mill didn't leave out any important details. That's a relief. Anyway, I'll be leaving in the morning," he said, taking another swig of his drink.

"Really?"

"Yes. We finished the book about an

hour ago. I have no reason to stay any longer," he said wryly.

"You don't honestly believe the lie that just came out of your mouth, do you?" she asked with a smirk.

His mouth gaped.

"Mel, we need another round of shots for the pool table," the waitress called over her shoulder as she passed with empty glasses.

"Coming up, Lynn." Turning back to him, she said, "Think about it for a minute. I'll be right back." She grabbed six shot glasses and a bottle of gold tequila, lined them up on the bar and expertly filled them to the brim without wasting a drop of expensive alcohol. She placed them on a tray for the waitress and turned her attention to Logan. "Well?"

He sighed. "No."

"So, why don't you stay? I mean, you're a writer. It's not like you have to rush back to the city, right?"

The fifth book released the following week, and the launch party was a big deal. His court case the following Monday morning was a much bigger deal. But he wasn't about to be a cliché and start telling his sorrows to the bartender. "It's complicated and besides, she doesn't want me to."

Melody hesitated, but then smiled sadly. "You're probably right about that."

That wasn't the pep talk he'd wanted. "Wow, you really know how to cheer a guy up."

"Sorry, it's in my nature to tell it how it is. My feet are firmly planted in reality and I don't believe in leading others to believe in fairy tales with disappointing endings."

For the first time he noticed she wasn't wearing a wedding band. "Divorced?"

"Widowed."

His track record for saying the wrong thing tonight must be at an all-time high. "I'm sorry."

Reaching for his glass, she refilled it and set it in front of him. "My husband died in a car accident almost three years ago. It's just that I know firsthand that real life never works out the way you plan it."

"Real life, no." When he first met Kendra, he'd thought they would be together forever. He certainly never thought they'd face off in court for custody of their child.

"Well, I appreciate you giving it to me straight."

"I mean, it couldn't hurt to tell her how you feel and see if it makes a difference."

"I did. It didn't." He shook his head. "I doubt she'll even want to say goodbye to me at this point."

"Leigh's upset with you?"

Logan nodded.

"Leigh never gets angry with anyone. What did you do?"

"Stuck my nose in her business where it didn't belong." He gave a wry laugh.

"I wouldn't worry about Leigh. She'll come around." She paused before adding, "But let me be the first to warn you—her grandmother Norris is another story. You do not want to mess with that woman or her family."

Leigh's grandmother. "Yeah, that warning is coming just a little too late."

WITH THE HURTFUL words still ringing in her ears, Leigh entered the nursery at the end of the hall and collapsed into the rocking chair. Scanning the room, she felt her mind reeling. Was she doing the right thing by adopting a child alone? Every child did deserve both a mother and a father.... She pushed the thought aside. What every child deserved was to be loved and cared for, and she could certainly offer that and much more.

She tried to tell herself that his words had come from a place of anger and hurt over his own fight for his family, but it was hard not to internalize it.

Worst of all, despite her disappointment over the way things had turned out that evening, the other thought plaguing her was the way his lips had felt pressed against her own. His kiss had come as a complete shock, despite the growing attraction she'd felt, as well. She'd never expected him to act on it. Not after he'd refused to kiss her before.

And she refused to entertain the what-if scenarios playing on repeat like an old cassette tape in her mind. After all, his reaction to her news hadn't exactly been accepting or warm. Resting her head against the cushion on the chair, she closed her eyes. What a mess. How had she let this happen?

She sat in the chair for a long time in the dark, the only light coming from the open butterfly-patterned curtains at the window. The gentle swaying of the chair helped to ease her tension. Everything would be fine. Logan would leave and life would go back to the way it had been. It had to and it would.

The ringing of her cell phone in her pocket, and the corresponding vibration made her jump. Logan? She glanced at the caller ID. The New Jersey Adoption Center. She checked the time above the flashing number. It was almost nine o'clock. Her heart pounded in her chest as she accepted the call. "Hello?"

"Leigh, it's Michelle Bennett."

"Hi."

"Sorry to call so late. I hope I'm not interrupting your evening."

No. Her evening had already been interrupted with an untimely kiss and harsh words all in a matter of moments from a man she was completely falling in love with and couldn't be with. She suspected that was too much to reveal, so she said simply, “I welcome a call anytime, Michelle. Is everything okay?”

Lise? Was she okay? Was the baby okay? Had she gone into labor? She stood and paced the hardwood floor.

“Everything is fine. But, Leigh, I’m afraid I have bad news.” The woman’s voice was strained.

Leigh’s hand shook violently on the phone and the lump in her throat prevented a response.

“Lise has decided to go with the other family.”

Her worst fears realized, Leigh fought to swallow past the lump that refused to go away.

“I’m so sorry, Leigh.”

Clearing her throat, she lowered herself back into the chair. “Did…um…did she say why?”

“I can tell you it was a very difficult decision for Lise. She went back and forth a number of times this afternoon before making a final decision…but, well—”

“You know what, don’t say any more.” Hearing a reason wouldn’t change the outcome and would only make her doubt her decision more.

"I can't tell you how incredibly sorry I am, Leigh."

"It's okay," she choked out. But it was far from okay. She'd gotten her hopes up so high this time it felt as though she were plummeting.

"I assure you, your file is on the top of our list…and if anything comes up—"

"I appreciate everything you've done, Michelle, thank you."

"Again, I'm sorry to have to give you this news. Good night, Leigh."

Leigh disconnected the call, allowing the phone to fall out of her hand as she leaned forward in an effort to stop the spinning.

Another child that wouldn't be hers.

CHAPTER TEN

LEIGH SCANNED THE menu items on the paper napkin at Joey's through swollen eyes, glancing through the front window every few seconds, waiting for her grandmother. Their Friday-morning early breakfast was usually one of her favorite parts of the week, but today she wasn't looking forward to seeing the older woman with her bloodshot eyes. Her grandmother knew her better than anyone, and she suspected her pain wouldn't go unnoticed. The night before had been one of the worst night's sleep she'd had in a very long time. Tossing and turning, she couldn't help wondering if she would ever have the family she longed for. And she fought against the nagging voice that wondered whether walking away from love in search of family was the right thing to do—it certainly sounded wrong.

"You ready to order, Leigh, or are you going to wait for Ginger?" April asked as she passed the booth.

"I'll wait, but a chamomile tea would be wonderful, thanks." What she really wanted was coffee, but she didn't think adding caffeine to her already anxious state was the way to go. Her hands were unsteady enough and the pounding in her temples would only be aggravated by the stimulant.

"Sure thing." The waitress disappeared behind the counter, poured the tea and returned, placing it on the table in front of Leigh. She lingered, twirling a strand of strawberry blond hair around her finger. She looked about to speak, then shook her head.

"Everything okay?"

The young woman took the question as an opportunity to dive into the booth across from her. "I'm fine. I'm worried about you. You look awful."

"Wow, thank you for that." Reaching up, she smoothed her hair.

"Yeah, that didn't help. Your hair is fine,

but your eyes look like you've been crying…a lot," she whispered.

Great. She shouldn't have left the house today. "I'm good, really. Just lack of sleep, that's all."

"So, everything is okay between you and Logan?"

There was no her and Logan, despite whatever the people in town might believe. "Of course. We were just working on his book together, that's all."

April looked disappointed. "Oh. That's too bad…. I thought—"

"You know, you can't believe everything you hear around town, April."

April stood as they saw Ginger come in. "Yeah, I guess the idea was kind of crazy, seeing as how he wasn't planning to stay long. He's such a great guy, though. It's really too bad he's leaving."

He was already gone. His truck had been gone from the parking lot of the Brookhollow Inn when she left that morning. She should feel relieved. After all, they had nothing left to say to each other…but she already missed him. Despite their argument and harsh words, she couldn't stop thinking about all he'd been asking. Give up everything here to follow him to California? She wasn't sure she could leave it all behind, even now that the adoption hadn't worked out. But the nagging voice in her mind kept asking the same question. Was what she had in Brookhollow worth losing everything she could have with Logan? She shook her head. It didn't matter now. He was gone.

"Who is leaving?" her grandmother asked, sliding into the booth across from her.

"Just Mr. Walters." Leigh hoped her dismissive tone sounded genuine. "How are you, Grandma?"

"Too old to still be running that bakery," Ginger said, shrugging out of her light jacket. Turning to April, she said, "I'll have a coffee please, dear." When April left, her eyes narrowed. "I knew this would happen."

Leigh pretended to scan the menu on the back of the paper placement. "Knew what would happen?"

"That you would be hurt when he left."

"What on earth gives you that idea?"

She forced a scoff before reaching for her tea.

"Other than your puffy, bloodshot eyes?"

She should have worn sunglasses. "I'm fine, Grandma."

Ginger stared at her for a long moment before saying, "Okay. It's your business. You know I'm not one to interfere." She picked up the menu and scanned the items.

Now it was Leigh's turn to stare incredulously. "Oh, really? *You* don't interfere?"

"Never."

"What about the discussion you had with Logan yesterday?"

"What?" She set the menu aside. "That was nothing. He came for raspberry muffins—before we even opened the store, by the way. I told him we didn't have any—"

"And then casually warned him not to break my heart?"

"Fine, I may have overstepped my boundaries a little...but I just wanted him to be realistic in his expectations of the outcome," her grandmother huffed.

"Grandma, what exactly did you think was happening?"

"You two were falling in love. Everyone in town could see it."

"That's ridiculous." The words held no conviction whatsoever. And why should they? They were a lie. They had been falling in love. She'd admitted as much to him only hours before. For the first time since her marriage had ended, she'd been tempted to take another chance at a relationship. Even if it meant making sacrifices.

"So you're going to be fine watching him go?"

"He's already gone and yes, I'm fine." Leigh forced herself to keep eye contact with the one woman who knew her better than anyone.

Ginger reached across the table and squeezed her hand. "You're not fine, not yet, but you will be. And I'm proud of you for not letting this thing with Logan derail your plans—unlike your mother did."

Leigh stiffened. "Grandma, Mom's happy. She and Dad love the life they lead." It always confused her that her grandmother was so hard on her mother. Her parents did extraordinary work. They were selfless, caring people who put others first.

"When your parents decided to become parents, *you* should have come first. Children should always be the priority. At least you understand that."

Her eyes filled with fresh tears.

"Sweet girl, believe me, this is really for the best. Love doesn't last—you know that firsthand—but this child—"

"Grandma, I'm not getting baby Ava. The birth mother chose the other family." She said the words quickly before her voice broke.

In a heartbeat, her grandmother had joined her on her side of the booth, her arms wrapped tightly around her.

Sitting there, not caring about the prying eyes, she wept for everything she'd lost in the arms of the one person she'd always been able to depend on.

LOGAN LEFT THROUGH THE front door of the Brookhollow Library. As promised, he'd stopped by to sign the copies of his novels that Kate had on the shelves. The signature wasn't perfect because of the cast, but she didn't seem to mind. He took a deep breath of the late October air and paused at the top of the stairs. Soon he would be back in the city and the peaceful serenity he'd experienced in the small town would be nothing but a sweet memory. He wished he could stay one more day. He hated that he was leaving before Halloween.

From where he stood, he could see signs in the storefront windows on Main Street boasting their evening candy distributing hours for the trick-or-treaters the following week.

The idea of being in town and not seeing Leigh was even more torturous than the idea of being miles away.

He was surprised to see the lights on at Ginger Snaps. It was just past ten o'clock and the bakery didn't open until noon on Fridays. He hesitated. He wondered if Leigh's grandmother had spoken to her yet since their argument and less than ideal parting the night before. He couldn't believe he'd said what he did. Hurting Leigh was the last thing he ever wanted to do, and his words had come from a place of his own suffering. Comparing Leigh's intentions with Kendra's had been more than unfair.

With or without a father, the baby Leigh was about to adopt would be the most loved and cared-for child in Brookhollow. He knew that without a doubt. He wished he could tell her, but his fear of making things even worse somehow stopped him.

The smell of the baked goods inside the bakery reached him three blocks away and, decision made, he headed toward the store. He was leaving, after all; the woman couldn't be that angry with him. At least he wouldn't be able to cause further damage. And besides, he owed her an apology. She'd been right to warn him and he wished he'd listened to her advice.

As he expected, the open sign was still turned to closed when he reached the front door. Maybe he should come back—he could wait until noon. He caught sight of Ginger through the window. What the hell? It was worth a shot. Maybe she'd be so relieved he was leaving that she'd actually let him in. As he knocked, the door moved. It was open. Well, if she didn't want people coming in when they were closed, she should really start locking the door, he mused.

Pushing the door open, he entered the warmth of the shop, savoring the delicious smells of cinnamon, pumpkin mixed with chocolate and coffee. He might need more than one bag.... He could freeze them.... Who was he kidding? In his state, he'd eat a dozen on the drive back to the city. "Hello," he called.

No reply.

Moving farther into the store, he peered around the counter. "Mrs. Norris?"

He waited for several long minutes at the counter, then called again. "Hello! I know the bakery's not open yet, but I'm on my way out of town..." The sound of a loud crash in the kitchen made him pause. "Ginger?"

When still no reply came, he lifted the gate in the counter and went back. Ginger Norris lay in a heap on the floor near the open oven a few feet away.

Oh no. This was not happening.

Motionless, he was relieved to see her chest rising and falling as he rushed toward her, taking his cell phone out of his pocket.

"Ginger?" he asked, kneeling on the floor beside her. "Can you hear me?" He dialed 911 without waiting for a response, and touched the woman's cheek. She felt cool, despite the heat in the kitchen, and her skin was damp. He checked her pulse—it was slow and weak. This wasn't good.

"Nine-one-one, do you have an emergency?"

"Yes, I'm at Ginger Snaps Bakery. The owner, Ginger Norris, appears to have had a heart attack, I think. She's lying on the floor of the kitchen unconscious."

"You found her that way?"

No, he knocked her out and then called emergency services. "Yes, of course."

"Okay…hold the line. I'm doing a search for Ginger Snaps in New York…" The operator's voice was annoyingly calm. This wasn't a 411 directory call—a sense of urgency would be nice. Wait, had she said New York?

"No, not New York, Brookhollow, New Jersey."

"I apologize, the number you are calling from is recognized as a New York number, sir."

He didn't care. "Brookhollow, New Jersey. Main Street, on the corner of… Oh, hell, I don't know…it's just Main Street."

"Don't worry, I've got your location, sir. Dispatch has been notified. What is your name?"

What did that matter? "Logan."

"Okay, Logan, I'm going to ask you a few questions. Is the patient male or female?"

Hadn't they covered that? "Female."

"Age?"

How old had Leigh said Ginger was? "Seventy-four, I think."

"And you say she's unresponsive?"

"That's right," he said, adjusting Ginger's head to rest on his knees while he supported the rest of her weight. He hated that she was on the dirty, hard concrete floor.

"Okay, can you feel a pulse? See a breath?"

He placed a hand on her neck. The pulse was faint, but it was there. "Yes and yes."

"Okay, just stay with her. The ambulance is on its way. I'll stay on the phone with you until the medical attendants arrive."

Stay with her. Of course he would stay with her—where else would he go? Sweat rolled down his forehead as he leaned over Ginger, not knowing what to do. Come on, everything in Brookhollow was thirty seconds away. What was taking so long?

A bell chimed on the oven and Ginger's eyes fluttered open. She tried to sit up.

He set his phone on the floor. "No, stay there...please." He put a hand on her arm to prevent her from moving too quickly.

"What are you doing here?" Panic rose in her voice. "What's happening?"

"Sir, are you there?" he heard the 911 attendant ask.

"Who's that?" Ginger glanced at the phone. "And why are you in my kitchen?"

"Sir?"

He ignored the phone. "I think you had a heart attack," he said to Ginger, keeping his voice calm. "I found you passed out in here..." He glanced at the clock on the microwave. "...about three minutes ago." Three minutes, that was all? It felt like three hours.

"I don't know what you're talking about. Get out." She stopped as her head swayed, and her hand went to her chest. Her face contorted in pain and she gasped for a breath.

"Ginger?" Where was the damn ambulance?

Her eyes closed and he caught her as she collapsed forward. Sitting on the floor beside her, he cradled her body in his arms, supporting her weight, a hand on her forehead as they continued the agonizing wait for the emergency service to arrive.

"Sir, is everything okay? Please respond," came from the phone on the floor, out of his reach.

"I'm kind of busy here," he yelled toward the phone.

A second later, the sound of the sirens brought immense relief, and then Logan cringed. Ginger Norris didn't seem like the type of woman who would appreciate a big scene. There would be no concealing her heart attack from the town's residents now with the wailing ambulance speeding down Main Street.

"I hear the ambulance. Do you require

further assistance?" the 911 attendant called through the phone.

As if she'd been much help at all. "We're good," Logan said.

Two paramedics were there a moment later with a stretcher and medical kit. Kneeling, the first, a young man who looked to be in his early twenties, lifted Ginger from Logan and laid her on her back on the floor. Logan quickly slid his good hand under her head to keep it off the hard flour-covered floor.

"What happened?" the man said, checking her pulse.

"I think it was a heart attack. I came by and found her on the floor and called 911. She gained consciousness once…then another attack—"

"Did she speak when she came to?"

"She yelled at me," Logan said.

The second young man nodded. "Sounds about right. Okay, let's get her into the ambulance." Kneeling, he slid his arms under Ginger's and hoisted her up onto the stretcher. The first young man secured his medical kit and fastened the straps around Ginger's legs.

Logan followed them outside, where they quickly secured the stretcher in the back of the ambulance. He watched as they attached an oxygen mask over her mouth and he was relieved to see her eyes open once more. Then shocked to see her reach out for him as her scared expression met his. "Can I ride with her?" he asked the attendant.

"Usually it would be just immediate family, but since you were there with her… sure, I don't think that's a problem."

Logan quickly climbed into the back of the ambulance and moved closer. He sat on the bench next to her as the driver shut the back doors and the ambulance pulled away from the curb. Tears streamed down the woman's face as she reached toward him, grasping his casted fingers.

"You're going to be okay," he said, wishing he knew that for sure. The woman looked as though she'd aged ten years in those few moments. Her skin looked gray and pale, and her eyes were tired.

Ginger clutched his injured hand in hers and he winced in pain but didn't pull his hand away.

She moved the mask. "You're still not getting any muffins," she said.

The woman was a fighter. "We'll see about that. Put your mask back on," he said, kissing the back of her hand.

LEIGH TAPPED HER foot impatiently and stared at the numbers lighting up in the elevator. The medical clinic in Brookhollow comprised three floors, but the ride to the top seemed to take forever. She wiped a tear from her cheek—they hadn't stopped pouring since she got the next-of-kin call twenty minutes earlier. After the night before and that morning, she couldn't believe she had any tears left. The past twenty-four hours had been the worst she'd endured in a long time. No Logan, no Ava and now... No, she wouldn't do that.

She forced a deep breath as the doors opened. Her grandmother was okay. She had to calm down. Her grandmother had been through enough; it wouldn't do any good to freak her out by her own anxiety. This time, her grandmother was relying on her to take the role of the strong one. Swiping at her cheeks, Leigh stepped from the elevator onto the quiet hospital floor. Her knees shook and her legs felt weak. Her stomach turned at the memory of the last time she'd been in this hospital, after her third miscarriage. That night, there'd been chaos, as the two doctors on duty had fought to save the life of her unborn child. But there had been nothing they could do then.

Reaching her grandmother's room, she pushed open the wooden, swinging door. Her eyes misted at the sight of her grandma, lying in the big bed, an oxygen tube coming from her nose and IV in her hand. Her grandmother hated hospitals and IVs. She refused to even visit a family doctor, instead relying on the monthly blood-pressure screenings at the fire hall to check her health. It was a miracle they'd gotten her here. Oh, why hadn't she insisted her grandmother take better care of herself? And working so much couldn't have helped. Well, things were going to change if...*when* she made it through this.

Moving farther into the room, Leigh couldn't remember seeing her grandmother so frail and helpless, and she coughed to clear her throat. Her grandmother's eyes opened and her head turned toward Leigh. A weak smile spread across her lips and she lifted a hand.

Taking it, she said, "Hi, Grandma." Her voice was barely more than a whisper as she smoothed the wispy gray strands of hair away from the older woman's face. Just hours ago, she'd been as vibrant and strong as ever.

Until she'd given her something to worry about with her news about the adoption. The guilt that washed over her was overwhelming.

Her grandmother strained to answer. "See, I told you I was getting too old to run the bakery." She coughed and sputtered as she tried to speak, but her voice crackled.

"Grandma?"

Ginger coughed again and her eyes widened in a look of fear as she struggled to catch her breath.

"Grandma, it's okay…just breathe." Where were the nurses? She searched the bedside table for the emergency button.

"They said the coughing is normal…

and that she may lose her voice. She's still weak."

Startled, she turned to face Logan. "What are you doing here?"

Logan came closer. "I was the one who found her, so the paramedics said I could come along."

"You called 911?" Logan had saved her grandmother's life. Who knew how long she could have been in there alone?

Ginger coughed again and clutched her chest.

"Are you okay, Grandma?"

"Water," she croaked.

"You stay with her. I'll get the nurse on duty and some water," Logan offered, disappearing in a flash.

Leigh nodded, clutching her grandmother's hand.

The nurse arrived in seconds. Leigh was grateful to see it was Lindsay Harper, Rachel's sister-in-law and a girl she'd gone to high school with. Lindsay might have a reputation for partying and gossip, but she was the best nurse on staff. "Ginger, you okay?" she asked. After handing her the water, she took Ginger's pulse and checked the IV bag.

Ginger nodded, resting her head back against the cushions. Her attempt to speak failed, so she just shook her head in frustration and let out a deep breath as she closed her eyes.

"She just needs rest. Dr. Harris says she should be cleared to go home in the morning after they run some tests this afternoon." Lindsay gave her a reassuring smile.

"What kind of tests?" Leigh asked quietly. If her grandmother heard they were planning to poke and prod at her, she'd check herself out immediately.

"Just some blood work and an EKG."

"Can I stay with her tonight?" The idea of leaving her alone turned her stomach. From now on she had to be there more for her grandmother, not the other way around.

"Sure. We'll have someone bring in a cot."

Leigh bit her lip, for the first time noticing her grandma's private room. There were only two such rooms in the clinic.

The others accommodated four per room. She wasn't sure why they'd placed Ginger in one, but the cost combined with the ambulance trip alone was going to cost them a small fortune. Self-employed, they didn't have medical insurance. A cot or any other luxuries would just add to the bill. Leigh eyed the chair Logan had vacated, noticing he hadn't returned with Lindsay. "The chair's fine. We'd like to keep the costs to a minimum." How many times had her grandmother said just that? She moved farther away and pulled Lindsay with her. "I'll cover the costs, just invoice me for… the room and ambulance…and anything else she needs."

Medication and tests were going to be additional costs. The money in her savings would cover everything. She'd just have to call the adoption clinic and put a hold on her application. She didn't give it a second thought. Decision made, she decided her grandmother would need her around more to help now anyway.

Lindsay waved a hand. "They're already being covered."

"By…?"

"Mr. Walters. He insisted and he said not to let you change anything. He said all invoices were to be sent to him in New York—now and for anything else Ginger may encounter." Lindsay's voice was firm as she repeated the instructions.

Logan was doing that for them? "But…I couldn't possibly let him."

"Look, I know you probably think he's done more than enough by saving's Ginger's life, but don't look a gift horse in the mouth, as the saying goes."

Leigh stood still, shock and confusion clouding her foggy mind. "Is that true? Logan saved her?"

With a glance toward the resting patient, Lindsay pulled her out of the room. Ginger's eyes were closed, but it was hard to tell if she was asleep. "The truth is, the paramedics say that her heart rate was dropping quickly. If Logan hadn't arrived when he did, then yeah, we could have lost her. You okay?" she asked, placing a hand on her shoulder.

"Yes," Leigh whispered.

"So, did you want the cot?"

"No." If the costs were being taken care

of by Logan, she didn't want them to be higher than absolutely necessary. The man had already done enough. He'd saved her grandmother's life.

"Okay. Well, here, he left this for you," she said, handing Leigh a folded medical-chart sheet.

Leigh unfolded it and the sight of the familiar chicken scratches made it hard to breathe. "Don't be stubborn. Get a cot and call if you need anything else. I'll stick around town, just in case you need me."

Unable to control her emotions any longer, she let a sob escape her lips.

Lindsay gave her a big hug. "It's been a rough morning, but she's fine. In a few days she'll be good as new."

Lindsay's words of encouragement did little to calm her fears, but she nodded as she pulled away. "Thanks, Lindsay."

Lindsay winked as she opened the door. "I'm not the one you should be thanking. I'll go get you that cot."

Leigh resumed her place in the chair next to her grandmother's bed, and a moment later the door behind her opened once more. “That was fast,” she said as she turned, then stopped. “Neil.”

“I came as soon as I heard,” he said, offering a quick hug, before turning his attention to Ginger.

Seeing him here at the hospital was the last thing she’d expected, but the feeling of support from him had a calming effect on her. “Thank you, but it really wasn’t necessary,” she said.

“Of course it was. We’re still family. How is she?” he asked quietly, so as not to disturb the sleeping woman.

We’re still family.... That caught her off guard. After years together, he was right; Ginger was someone who meant a lot to him. “She did have a heart attack, and they’re keeping her overnight to run a few tests.”

His eyes widened. “Does she know that yet?”

Leigh shook her head. “I figure I’ll let the doctor tell her.”

“Probably best.” He nodded. “Dumb question, but how are you holding up?” He reached for her hand and squeezed it. It was the first time they’d been alone together since the divorce, and this was definitely the most intense moment they'd shared. Strangely enough, all she felt was comfort from his presence.

"I'll be okay. I'm staying with her tonight."

He lowered his voice as he said, "Look, I want to apologize about Angela. I keep telling her to stop asking you to watch the kids, but she insists you're the only person she trusts to watch them."

"I'm sorry, Neil. I just don't know—"

"You don't have to explain. I understand why you can't do it. And I don't want you to stress over it, okay? You have enough on your plate, especially now. Leave Angela to me," he said.

For the first time, the idea of watching his children didn't seem so terrible. *We're still family,* he'd said. Maybe it was his words or maybe it was just his being there when she needed a friend and a hug, but all of a sudden moving forward as friends seemed a lot easier. She could do this for him, couldn't she? "You know what… um…I'll be hiring Ashley full-time in the new year, so I'd love to offer the space to the kids."

"Really? Are you sure?" He didn't look convinced. "It's a lot to ask."

"It's okay, really. But, I'll warn you—I only have space for three, so please stop having children."

He nodded with a smile. "Understood. Thanks, Leigh. So, I…uh…saw Logan leaving just now."

"He was the one who found Grandma. He called the ambulance," she said, so grateful that he'd been there when he was.

"Oh, wow. Well, I guess I probably shouldn't tell you how much he annoys me."

Leigh's smile was the first one she'd been able to muster since receiving the news about her grandmother. "He has a way of growing on you," she said, fighting the tightening in her chest.

"As long as you're happy." Neil shifted uncomfortably and Leigh just nodded, unable to tell him that in the past twenty-four hours, she'd struggled to find even a glimpse of happiness.

"If you need anything at all, don't hesitate to call us," he said, kissing her cheek as he let himself out.

"Thank you," she said, watching him leave.

From across the room, her grandmother said, "And I thought my heart attack was the unexpected part of the day."

UPON OPENING HIS eyes the following morning, Logan felt a moment of panic. He hadn't heard anything from Leigh at all the day before after leaving her at the medical clinic and he'd struggled to catch pieces of information from others as he wandered around town feeling helpless. This hadn't exactly been the way he'd been hoping to extend his stay in Brookhollow.

Rolling out of bed, he wrapped his cast in a plastic grocery bag and stepped into a hot shower. Images of Ginger Norris lying on the floor of her bakery had repeated in his mind, and his few hours of sleep had been plagued with disturbing, nonsensical nightmares. He just hoped the woman recovered well and fast. He knew how much she meant to Leigh. He'd shut off the water when the room phone rang. Leigh? Tossing a towel around his waist, he rushed to answer. "Hello?"

"Hi, Mr. Walters. Sorry to bother you, but, well, there's a reporter from the *Brookhollow View*, the local newspaper, here. She's asking for a few minutes of your time." Victoria Mason sounded apologetic.

"Why?"

"You're kind of the talk of the town, being the local hero and all."

"Seriously?" Logan sighed. "Will she leave if I say no?" The last thing he wanted was thanks or praise or worst of all—publicity for helping the woman. He'd left New York to keep a low profile, and here he'd created a buzz in the small town without meaning to. He'd simply done what anyone else in the town would have in his situation.

"Honestly, probably not. Did you want me to try?"

"No, that's fine. Tell her I'll be right down." Logan replaced the receiver and ran a hand over his stubbly chin. The local media? Now what had he gotten himself into? "No good deed goes unpunished," he mumbled, reaching for his jeans.

CHAPTER ELEVEN

"…THE AUTHOR WITH the broken wrist then proceeded to call 911 and stayed with the injured woman until the ambulance arrived…." Rachel read from the *Brookhollow View,* following Leigh into her kitchen. "Have you read this yet?"

"Yes," Leigh said. A number of times. Each time her heart had swelled with the knowledge that if he hadn't been there…

"What an amazing man," Rachel said, sitting at the table. They'd just finished bringing in Ginger's items and setting them in the spare guest room where the doctors and Leigh had insisted she stay for at least a few nights while she recovered. The older lady lay on the couch in the living room asleep, still determined that after a quick nap, she was heading home. "And to think we all thought he was grumpy… and rude."

"He *was* grumpy and rude in the beginning," Leigh pointed out, though she didn't for a second believe it. Logan was neither grumpy nor rude. He was caring and kind and in love with her. And apparently still in Brookhollow. Next door.

Leigh poured two cups of raspberry-flavored hot chocolate and carried them to the table. "Fine, I'll admit it…we were all wrong about him."

"And…?" Rachel pressed.

"And he's actually very kind and caring."

"You're forgetting handsome, smart, generous…"

She wasn't forgetting. She just didn't want to acknowledge any more of Logan's good attributes. The day before, being angry with him had given her a reason to distance herself, to put up a barrier between them. His unintentionally hurtful words had given her something to go back to whenever her heart started pounding at the thought of him. Now she had nothing.

Nothing left to protect her open heart from the pain of his leaving. "I've noticed."

"So, what are you going to do about it?" Rachel asked, sipping her hot chocolate.

"Nothing." Leigh said the painful words with a shrug. "I mean, what can I do? He'd be gone by now if Grandma hadn't gone into the hospital yesterday." She lowered her gaze to her cup and toyed with the glass handle. "Besides, if he doesn't get custody of his daughter next week, he's moving to L.A."

"Now that the adoption hasn't happened, you could go with him." Rachel's words echoed Logan's sentiment and the reoccurring thoughts she'd had herself.

Leigh shook her head. "I have the day care…and now Grandma. Here." There was no way she could move to L.A. and leave her grandmother now that her health was failing.

"Okay, well, what if he does get custody?"

She refused to get her hopes up just to have them shattered again. No, it was best to let Logan leave and get on with her life, her responsibilities…her loneliness and longing for a family. "I can't even think about any of this right now," she said, hearing her grandmother call from the other room.

"Okay..." Rachel sighed as she stared at the photo of Logan in the paper. "I just hate that once again, everything you've always wanted is just slightly out of reach. It's not fair."

Rachel was right. It wasn't fair, but no one ever promised life would be.

THE RINGING CELL phone in his hand was a sense of torment as Logan glanced around the room at the Brookhollow Inn for a final time the following morning. Everything was packed and near the door, ready to go...but he couldn't bring himself to leave. Yet the still-Δ3unanswered call from Clive reminded him of one of the many important reasons he had to get back to the city. On the last ring, he answered. "Hey, Clive. I know the ending wasn't exactly what I'd outlined in the synopsis, but—"

"*New York Times* bestselling author saves local bakery owner," Clive said into the phone, interrupting the long list of explanations he had for the abrupt change in his series ending. “Logan Walters rescues a woman having a heart attack just days before his long-awaited comeback with the release of *Dark Heart,* the fifth book in his Van Gardener series—an act of altruism or a publicity stunt?”

What? Seriously? “Where are you reading that?” Logan asked through a groan, rubbing the back of his neck. How had the story made its way to Clive in New York? He hadn’t expected the *Brookhollow View* to have an online version.

“The *New York Post*...the *Times*...you name it, the story’s there. What are you doing in that small town, Logan? Have you forgotten why you’re there? Actually scratch that. Better question—have you forgotten you’re a writer, not a superhero?”

Good question. “That story was supposed to only have been published locally. I had no idea it was being leaked to the city papers.” Logan sat on the edge of his bed. So much for keeping a low profile until book five in his series released the following week. He searched his mind, trying to remember exactly what he’d said to the reporter of the *Brookhollow View.* In his tired, anxious state the previous morning, he hoped he hadn't said anything stupid.

"I think you're missing the point. Should I even ask if the book got finished? I'm meeting with Winston Brooks tomorrow, but even with this article and your local hero status, I'm not sure I can get another extension, Logan."

His editor, Winston Brooks, had been the one to convince H and S Publishing to consider his series again after his long absence. The man was a fantastic editor and Logan was happy to be able to say, "It's done. Didn't you get the file I sent last night?" He'd spent the day in his room at the B & B, doing a final edit on the manuscript while sitting next to the window hoping for any sign of Leigh.

"Yes, but I thought you were messing with me, so I didn't open it. Seriously?" Clive's relief eased some of the tension. "You mean it's done? Early?"

"Yes, man. What do you think I've been doing out here all this time?" Logan asked sarcastically.

"After seeing this article today, I

wouldn't even hazard a guess. So you're home—here in the city?"

"Not yet."

"On your way back?"

"Sort of, yeah…I'm leaving here shortly." He should have been back in the city by now. He wasn't sure why he'd stayed the extra day. Clearly, Leigh and her grandmother were fine. They didn't need him. He'd just wanted to be sure. But now, two days and no word from Leigh couldn't be any more clear. She didn't want to see him or talk to him. Probably easier for everyone, but the realization still hurt.

"Great, see you when you get here," Clive was saying. "Oh, and, Logan?"

"Yeah?"

"Don't lose sight of what's important… No more distractions, okay?"

What *was* important? Securing this comeback to gain footing for his court case…winning the court case so he could continue to raise his daughter and not have to move to L.A…to maybe convince Leigh to give them a chance? How connected everything was, yet one broken link would negatively affect everything that was important. "I'll see you soon," Logan said, disconnecting. Picking up his coat from the chair, he did a final scan of the room and headed for the door. No sense putting off leaving any longer. He swung it open and paused. "Leigh?"

"Hi," she said, hand poised to knock.

"Hi." Man, she was a sight for sore eyes. He had been missing her badly for the last few days, but he hadn't even realized just how much until she was standing right there in front of him.

She eyed the bags on the floor near the door. "You're leaving now?"

"Yeah. Sorry, I was going to come say goodbye, see how Ginger was feeling."

"Were you?"

She did know him well. "No, I wasn't. I was going to sneak out of here as fast as I could, before I said or did something to hurt you again," he said, lowering his voice as a couple of inn guests walked passed them in the hall. Now was his final opportunity to say something right, to apologize. "Leigh, I am so sorry for what I said the other night. I was wrong. You're going to make a terrific mother and that baby will be lucky to have you."

She shook her head. "The birth mother decided on the couple."

He couldn't believe it. "Oh, Leigh, I'm so incredibly sorry...." He enveloped her in a hug. He squeezed her tight, breathing in the scent of her jasmine shampoo. She'd been through so much. And now her grandmother wasn't well. When were things supposed to get easier for her?

"It hadn't been a certainty anyway." She moved away from him.

"Which is why you kept it to yourself." He understood now and he felt even worse for forcing her secret out of her.

She nodded. "Anyway, I wanted to say thank you again for being at the bakery yesterday and for everything else."

"I'm just glad I'd been there. In all honesty, I went with the intention of doing battle with Ginger for some muffins," he said, unable to resist touching her cheek.

She smiled and, reaching behind her in the hallway, she picked up a paper bag and handed it to him. "She said to give you these."

He didn't have to open it to know what was inside. "And all I had to do was save her life," he said with a smile of his own.

"I also wanted to let you know that I really appreciate your offer to pay the medical costs, but I can't let you do that."

"They're already taken care of," he said firmly. "Consider it payment for your story assist, if that makes it easier."

"I said payment wasn't necessary."

"Leigh, please give me the satisfaction of knowing I was able to help make things even a little bit easier, okay?"

He could see her struggle with her pride, but she finally nodded. "Okay. Thank you, Logan."

"Anything for you," he said, his voice barely above a whisper.

They stood like that in silence for several moments. "Well, I won't keep you any longer. Um…thank you again, and I really am sorry about your wrist."

"Falling off that ladder was the best thing that could have happened to me," Logan said.

"I seriously doubt that."

Logan rested his hands on her shoulders.

"Okay, maybe not falling off the ladder, but meeting you was." He stared into her brown eyes.

"I'll miss you," she whispered, dropping her eyes.

Lifting her chin, he gently stroked her cheek. "What if I want to see you again?" New York, L.A.—it didn't matter. Other couples made the long-distance thing work.

"Once you get back to the city, you'll be busy with your book release and the court case."

"When I got here, I couldn't wait to finish this book and get on with my life…then you and that ladder changed everything. Now this court case just got even more important to win so I can keep Amelia and make a home with her here."

"Why is it that everything I want in life always rests in the hands of someone else?"

"That doesn't have to happen with us…. Make the decision yourself to be with me. Wherever that is."

She shook her head. "I can't make that

choice right now, Logan. With Grandma being sick…"

"So what happens with us, then? I'll see you when I see you? Someday? Never?" His voice was raw with emotion as he choked out the words.

Leigh raised a hand to his face and standing on tiptoes, she placed a kiss on his cheek. "My choice would be someday, definitely someday."

CHAPTER TWELVE

"To the completion of the series." Clive Romanis held his shot glass in the air above the table at LexBar in Manhattan the following evening. The after-work crowd was trickling in for appetizers and cocktails, and Logan and his agent had arrived early to secure their usual table.

Logan lifted his tequila shot. Tossing his head back, he drained the contents and set the glass on the table. He relaxed against the plush red velvet seats along the window, enjoying the heat radiating from the fireplace in the corner. Winter had arrived early in the city, and the trees outside that had once boasted colorful leaves when he'd left for Brookhollow were now bare and the sidewalk was covered in a thin layer of frost as evening fell on New York.

"You did it, man." Clive shook his head.

"I have to say, over the years I've never lost faith in you...but these last few months..."

"I know. And I appreciate your support," Logan said, scanning the bustling hot spot. The watering hole used to be his favorite place to just sit, observe and write into all hours of the morning. Countless evenings had been spent watching human behavior in the dimly lit bar, where things seemed to get more intriguing with each drink and each passing hour. But now he longed for the friendly neighborhood bar in Brookhollow, or the bustling diner on Main Street or more than anything else, the gazebo in the backyard of the bed-and-breakfast.

He checked his watch. It was just past eight, but already he wanted to call it a night. Though he suspected the loneliness he felt would only follow him wherever he went. He checked his phone—no calls.

"You okay, buddy?" Clive asked. "I thought you'd be more excited to have the book submitted to the publisher. You can finally move on to something else."

"Yeah...no...you're right."

"You *are* thinking about your next project, right? I mean we didn't make this comeback just for you to slink away again, right?"

Logan knew Clive asked out of concern, that it was more than the big paycheck his work attracted. His agent was his friend and he cared about him. He wanted him to continue doing what he loved.

"Of course. I just need to focus on the court case next week, let my hand heal some more. But once the cast is off, I'll be right back at it."

"Great," Clive said as his cell phone vibrated on the table next to him. Smiling, he answered it, hitting the button for speakerphone. "Gina, pretty lady, how are you?"

"Besides working late on this last-minute release party for you?" she answered sweetly. Clive, like his writer client, often left things to the last minute, driving their public-relations department crazy.

"Be nice, you're on speakerphone. Logan's here."

"Hi, Logan. Congrats on the book release," Gina said.

"Thanks, Gina."

"Anyway, Clive, the venue is booked

for Saturday night. Ella's Lounge at eight o'clock will be on the invite. Full catering provided by Carla's Bistro."

"No shellfish," Clive said.

The man had the most serious allergic reaction to shellfish Logan had ever seen.

"Trust me, no one wants to see your face swell like Eddie Murphy's in a fat suit.... What was that movie?"

"The Nutty Professor," Logan said.

Gina laughed. "That's the one. Creepy."

"All right, enough," Clive said. "Anything else, Gina?"

"Yes, cash bar or open?" she asked.

"Open," Clive answered with a grin. "Logan's advance should cover it."

"Gina, make sure the bistro throws in a few shrimp trays," Logan said.

She laughed. "I'll see what I can do. Usual guest list?"

"Yes," Clive said.

"Um...actually...Gina, there's another person I'd like to invite." Logan knew she wouldn't attend, but he had to invite her. Give her the opportunity to say no. And if she did show up...he wouldn't even give himself the false hope.

"No problem. Just text me the name and address, and I'll send the invite right away. Anything else, Clive, or can I go home now?" she asked with a yawn.

"That's it. I appreciate your work, Gina."

"Whatever. Remember this at bonus time," she said, disconnecting the call.

Clive set the phone aside and studied Logan. "So, who is she?"

"Who's who?"

"The mysterious extra guest."

"No one you know," Logan said with a shrug as he texted Gina Leigh's name and address in Brookhollow.

"Let me guess…"

"No."

"It's that woman who helped you type the manuscript, isn't it? Linda?"

"Leigh," Logan started to say, but, her name stuck in his throat. Not hearing from her had been torture. What did he expect? He couldn't expect her to put her plans on hold while he sorted his life out.

"Do you think she'll come?" Clive asked, flagging down their waitress for the bill.

"No," Logan answered honestly.

"So why invite her?" His agent slid the bill his way.

Logan opened his wallet and placed his credit card on the table. "Because I want to give her the opportunity to not show up."

LEIGH CLOSED THE door to the guest room after checking on her grandmother. Almost a week since the heart attack and Ginger was feeling much better. Her appetite had returned and she'd returned to the bakery, but her shifts were short and she was still tired a lot. It was almost eight o'clock and normally she would have already been at the bakery for hours, but despite her request to be woken at six, Leigh had let her sleep. She'd deal with her wrath later if it came. Though in the past few days, her grandmother had seemed mellower, more accepting of her own limitations.

The doorbell rang and Leigh went to answer it. Opening it, she smiled as she saw Melody Myers and her twin boys on the porch step. "Hi, guys."

Melody rubbed her arms as she danced from one foot to the other behind the kids.

"It's freezing out here." She glanced toward the dark clouds in the early morning sky. "If I didn't know any better, I'd swear it was about to snow."

"Come on inside and warm up," she said.

"I'd love to…but if I shut off the van, it may not start again." She checked her watch. "Besides, my shift at Play Hard Sports starts in an hour. Thank you again for watching them today. I swear, I can't remember there being this many PD days when we were in school."

"No, you and Pat just skipped class on your own," Leigh said with a smile. Melody and her late husband had been known for their skipping class to hang out and record new music in Patrick's homemade recording studio.

"You and Dad cut class?" Josh's eyes were wide.

"Awesome, that means you can't get mad at us when we do it," David added.

Melody shot Leigh a look.

"Sorry, Mel. I forgot—little ears."

Melody ushered the boys inside past Leigh. "Ah, don't worry about it. I'm raising athletes, not scholars. They take after their parents when it comes to school, I'm afraid. By the way, is Mr. Walters still here? I haven't seen him around."

Melody had met Logan? "He left earlier this week." Leigh prayed her tone sounded nonchalant.

"That's too bad. I wanted to thank him again for all of his help. I got an A on my Play Hard Sports management test last week."

"Logan had something to do with that?"

"He helped me study. The other night at the bar—the night you were mad at him." Melody clamped her lips tight. "Anyway, I was having trouble with memorizing a bunch of incredibly boring definitions. He helped by quizzing me."

"Oh," Leigh said. "That's really great. Congrats, Mel."

"I have to say, I'm not a fan of very many people, but he was kind of great," she said, zipping her coat higher as a gust of wind whipped past them. "Sure made an impact on people around here."

"It certainly seems that way." All Leigh

knew for sure was that he'd made an impact on her. A big one.

"DYLAN, PLEASE PUT YOUR hat back on," Leigh said to the little boy, shivering in the late morning air. The wind whipped through her own fall jacket and she pulled her hood up to block the cold breeze from hitting her cheeks. These morning walks to the mailbox with the kids would be coming to an end now that the weather was getting so much colder. She didn't remember last November second being this cold. Though she suspected she said that every year.

Behind her, the kids threw leaves at one another as she opened her mailbox and took out a handful of envelopes. Bills, flyers…and a white, gold-embossed envelope with her name written in script across the front. The return address in the top left-hand corner was a public relations firm in New York City. Unable to wait until they were back inside, Leigh locked the mailbox and tore open the envelope as she led the kids back toward the day care.

Her eyes flew across the embossed

lettering on the invitation and her pulse raced. Logan was inviting her to the book-release party for book five in the series, the one she'd already preordered and was waiting eagerly to read.

She'd finished the first four in record time, reading late into the night every evening. While the books were suspenseful and often chilling, she couldn't put them down, craving word after word, knowing they'd come from Logan. She'd traced her hand along the book covers, somehow feeling he was there when she was alone with the words she knew were painstakingly a part of him. And though the back cover images looked nothing like the man she'd fallen in love with, she'd spent more time than she'd ever admit staring at them.

"What is that, Miss Leigh?" Melissa asked, peering over her arm as she ushered them inside a moment later.

"An invitation," she answered, laying it aside to help the kids with their coats. Reaching into the closet, she grabbed several hangers and handed them to the children.

"To a party?" David asked, kicking his boots into the closet.

"Sort of." Leigh nodded, picking up the invitation again. Ella's Lounge in New York. She'd never been, but Victoria talked about it all the time as one of her favorite places in Manhattan.

The last time she'd been to the city was to visit the fertility-treatment center there. At the time, an evening out hadn't exactly been on the agenda.

"My dad buys me a new dress when we go to parties. Are you going to buy a new dress, Miss Leigh?" Melissa asked.

"Oh, I'm not sure I'm going." Leigh desperate to act nonchalant, led the kids into the kitchen for their morning snack. Of course she wouldn't go. What would be the point? She'd send a card to congratulate him—that was good enough.

The man saved your grandmother's life and a card is good enough? She sighed.

"Definitely not going to go," she muttered, unwrapping the banana bread she'd made the night before. She opened the cupboard and retrieved a stack of multicolored plastic plates, placing a slice on each and handing them to the kids sitting at the table.

"Why not?" Dylan asked, picking up his banana bread and taking a big bite.

"Why not? Let's see. Well, it's in New York," Leigh explained, pouring their milk.

"How far is that?"

"About a three-hour drive…if traffic is good."

"That's not that far. We drive seven hours to Boston to visit Grandma and Grandpa every second weekend," Isabel said.

Pulling out a chair, Leigh sat at the table and reached for a slice of the banana bread. "That's different. Visiting your grandparents is important."

"Whose party is it?" Melissa asked.

"Mr. Walters. Remember, the writer who was visiting? The man who helped us decorate the lawn for Halloween."

Melissa's eyes took on a dreamy glaze as she nodded. "He was cute."

"He was almost forty years old," Leigh said with a laugh. Besides, *handsome* would be the word she would use.

"He rescued me."

"He was a nice man." It appeared Logan had made quite an impact on everyone during his short visit.

"He didn't hang your sign, though," Dylan said. "And he had a scruffy beard."

"That's true." Leigh suppressed a laugh. Was she really pro-and-conning the decision of whether to attend the book release party with input from three four-year-olds?

"If you do go, who will look after us? Ashley?" Isabel asked, eyes wide.

"I would only be gone for the day—on the weekend. I'd be back by Monday morning." After having said goodbye to Logan once again. She didn't relish the prospect. Standing, she poured a cup of chamomile tea and took a sip. "Anyway, I don't think I'm going to go."

She tossed the invitation on the stack of mail in a tray on her counter. What would be the point? Seeing Logan for one more night wasn't enough, she knew that now. In the few days that he'd been gone, she'd missed him more and more with each passing minute. Missed his crazy sense of humor, his tiny chicken scratch, impossible-to-read writing, the way he looked at her and made her feel alive. Yes, definitely missed that last one the most.

LEIGH SAT IN the sitting room on Friday evening, the invitation in her hand. The past few days she'd spent more time than she would admit staring at the gold-embossed lettering stuck to her fridge and thinking about what it meant. Had he invited her just to be polite? Did he really want to see her again? Saying goodbye once had been hard enough.

"Hello?" Her grandmother Norris's voice drifted through the house.

"In the sitting room, Grandma." Leigh hid the invitation under a copy of Logan's book on the end table and stood to hug her grandmother as she came in. Since the heart attack, her grandmother's strength was returning more each day. However, she *had* agreed to start looking for an extra hand for the bakery to reduce her shifts and not be there alone. "How are you feeling?"

"Like it's time for me to go home." The older woman shivered, wrapping her cardigan sweater around her as she sat in the chair closest to the fireplace.

"There's no rush, Grandma," she said. The idea of her grandmother being alone in her apartment above the bakery terrified her. What if she had another attack? And, left to her own devices, would she stick to her promise of reduced shifts?

"I'm leaving in the morning. That's final," she said, tucking a blanket around her legs on the couch. "But don't worry, I've decided maybe it's time to move into the seniors' complex. All of my friends are there anyway."

Seniors' complex? This didn't sound like Ginger. Her grandmother had claimed she'd never get *that* old. The heart attack had clearly frightened her more than she'd revealed. "You don't have to do that. You can stay here."

"No way. You have your own life to worry about."

Leigh sighed. "Any point in arguing?"

"None." Ginger unfolded a quilt on the back of the sofa and draped it over her shoulders. "It's cozy in here." She changed the subject, and Leigh knew to let the subject drop. Once her grandmother made a decision, she stuck to it.

"This is my favorite room in the house."

Her grandma noticed the book on the table and picked it up. "This one of his books?"

"Yes. It just came out today. I finished the other four earlier this week."

"You were always an avid reader, but that seems a little fast even for you," Ginger said with a knowing look.

"His writing is fascinating, that's all," Leigh said with a shrug.

Ginger turned the book over in her hands and stared at the picture of Logan on the back cover. "He is handsome."

She nodded. He was handsome, but more important, he was kind and smart, and thoughtful. As the days passed, she craved the sight of him, the sound of his voice more and more, and reading his books was the closest thing to being with him she could get.

Unless of course she went to New York that weekend. But then what? One night and then she was right back where she was now.

Ginger picked up the invitation on the table. She fingered the embossed lettering. "Beautiful invitation."

"Mmm-hmm," Leigh said, forcing her voice to remain steady.

"His world must be very exciting in the city. These parties with fantastic people, dining with agents and editors…a totally different life, really."

"Mmm-hmm," was all she could think to reply.

"Are you planning to attend?"

"Every other thought—yes," Leigh answered quietly, honestly.

"Then those are the thoughts you should listen to. Not the ones holding you back." Her grandmother stood and sat on the arm of her chair. She wrapped an arm around her.

"I thought you didn't like him."

"I liked him just fine. More so after he saved my life, obviously."

Leigh laughed. "Obviously."

"I just wanted what was best for you," Ginger said, handing her the invitation.

"That's not him." Maybe if she said it enough, it would eventually be true.

"Well, it's certainly not anyone else. I see that now."

CHAPTER THIRTEEN

LOGAN LAY STARING at his bedroom ceiling, unable to sleep. The early-morning dawn burst through the cracks in the blinds, and the sounds of the city came through the walls of his studio apartment on Lexington Avenue. His cell-phone calendar chimed and he didn't need to look to know what the reminder said—Book Release Party. A day for celebrating an accomplishment, a day to enjoy his returning success. But what value did it hold when he was alone? He'd initially returned to the series for the same reason he'd started writing in the first place, to help fill a void, to provide an escape from his struggles. But now he realized it didn't matter how many books he wrote, or how many hours were spent forgetting about the pain; it was always there when he wrote the last word.

Pushing back the sheets, he swung his long legs over the side of his bed and sat there with his elbows on his knees, contemplating his day. He had all day to himself…to think about Leigh.

Shaking his head, he forced himself up. Pulling on his jeans and a hooded sweatshirt, he descended the stairs from his loft bedroom to the open-concept kitchen and living room. Opening the cupboard, he sighed. No coffee. Knowing he couldn't focus on anything until there was a Starbucks cup in his hand, he grabbed his wallet and keys from the kitchen counter, shoved his feet into his running shoes and left the apartment.

Ten minutes later, he inhaled the smell of the coffee as he scanned the display case.

"Can I get you anything?" the young barista asked, opening the back of the display.

"Um…do you have any raspberry muffins?" His own, the parting gift from Ginger Norris, had disappeared earlier that week. His attempt at freezing them fell short after the first lonely bite the first night back in his cold, dark apartment.

"No, sorry…just bran or oatmeal."

"Only the coffee, then," he said, reaching into his pocket for his wallet.

"Hadn't seen you in here for a while," the young woman said with a smile as she punched in his usual coffee.

"I was away for a few weeks." He hadn't even thought she'd ever noticed him. He usually came in during the early-morning rush, and there was no time for idle chit-chat.

"What happened to your hand?" she asked, handing him the coffee.

"Fell off a ladder."

"That sucks. Aren't you a writer?"

Her question surprised him. "Yeah, did I mention that before?" It wasn't something he usually announced.

"No, but I noticed you in here writing on yellow legal-pad paper a few weeks ago."

He did sometimes go there to work if his apartment got too quiet. "Oh."

"What do you write?" she asked.

"Mystery novels."

"Ever published anything?"

"Actually my fifth novel released yesterday." He wasn't sure why he said it, but the girl seemed genuinely curious. He missed friendly conversation since leaving Brookhollow.

"That's great, congratulations. What are you doing to celebrate?" she asked, pushing his money away. "It's on the house. Consider it a book-release gift."

"Thank you. Well, my book-release party is this evening. Until then..." He shrugged.

Another customer approached the counter and he moved aside, putting his money back in his wallet. The Cutler desk ad from Danielle O'Connor fell out and he bent to pick it up. He suspected it was probably sold by now.

"Well, make sure you reward yourself for the accomplishment," the barista said, turning her attention to the next customer.

"Thanks," Logan said, glancing at the ad again. Reward himself. Well, there were really only three things he wanted—Amelia, Leigh and this desk. He sighed. There was nothing he could do about the first two at the moment. Reaching into his pocket, he dug out his cell phone, punching in the Boston area number. If he was forced to move to L.A., he'd find a way to take it with him.

LOGAN LEANED AGAINST the bar at Ella's Lounge at 7:58 that night, having barely made it on time. The drive to Boston and back had taken the greater part of his day, but he was now the proud new owner of the Cutler rolltop desk he'd always wanted. The distraction of the road trip and the excitement of finally having it in his possession did help to liven his mood, but now sweat dripped down his forehead in the crowded bar and his stomach was in knots. Two more minutes until he had to get up to the microphone and thank everyone for coming, read an excerpt from his book and answer questions. Two more minutes until he had to admit to himself what he'd known all along: she wasn't coming. What they'd had in Brookhollow would remain there and in his memory.

"Logan? We're ready to get started," Gina said behind him.

Turning, he forced all thoughts of Leigh

from his mind. He just had to get through this few hours. "Okay, just give me a second."

"Whenever you're ready," Gina said, moving away to inform the crowd they were ready to begin the reading.

Logan took a deep breath, drained the contents of his glass and turned. His breath caught in his throat as he saw Leigh, standing near the door. He blinked. Smiling, she held up a hand in greeting, and in a daze Logan made his way to where she stood, seemingly frozen to the spot.

"Hi," he said.

"Hi."

"I didn't think you'd come." She was here. He couldn't believe it.

"Honestly, me, neither."

"I'm glad you did," he said, touching her bare arm. In the black V-neck, A-line dress, she looked amazing. She wore her hair in soft curls around her shoulders with a pale pink lipstick on her lips. The memory of how safe and welcoming those lips had felt pressing against his only a week ago made him forget where he was and he stepped closer. Only a week ago, yet it felt like a lifetime. "I've missed you," he whispered, unfazed by the hundreds of curious onlookers. This might not be a small town, but rumors would still fly. He didn't care.

He watched her swallow hard and her cheeks flushed. "I missed you, too. Turns out, I was wrong—not everything I needed was in Brookhollow."

"That's funny, because until now, everything I needed was."

"Logan, we're ready for you," Gina said, coming up behind him. Noticing Leigh, she smiled. "Sorry to drag him away, but his adoring fans await."

Logan rolled his eyes. He hadn't felt like going through with this release party all day and now that Leigh was here, he just wanted to take her back to his apartment, wrap his arms around her.... How long was she staying? "You'll stay right here? I'll read fast...maybe skip over a bunch of boring stuff."

Leigh nodded. "Of course. This is your night. Do your thing." She removed his hand from her arm and gave him a small shove.

"Thanks. You can have him back in

twenty minutes," Gina said, taking his elbow and leading him toward the stage.

"Stay," Logan mouthed, glancing back over his shoulder. Now that she was here, he was terrified she would leave before he got the chance to tell her everything he should have before.

LEIGH WATCHED AS Logan was escorted by the petite, trendy blonde with the six-inch stilettos and twenty-two-inch waist, fighting a sense of jealousy. Brushing it aside, she scanned the room for an empty seat as Logan took the microphone on stage. Sliding into a booth along the back wall, she looked around the sophisticated bar. It had been a long time since she'd been in the city and she'd forgotten how fast-paced and exciting it could be. She ran a hand along the plush velvet seat and took in the elegantly dressed tables. So different from anything in Brookhollow. The Fireside Grill was the closest thing to fine dining they had and it didn't come close.

Glancing down at her long dark velvet dress and simple heels, she felt an uncomfortable nervousness creeping down her spine as she noticed the curious stares from the neighboring tables. Prada and Hugo Boss filled the crowded room. Logan's sophisticated friends and colleagues in their expensive jewelry. Art-world elegance. Her heart raced and she reached unsteadily for the water carafe to fill an empty wineglass in front of her. Her mouth was dry and her palms were damp. What was she doing here? While Logan fit so easily into her world, she stuck out like a sore thumb in his. And it would be so much worse in L.A.

Not that she was considering L.A.

Was she?

She raised the glass to her lips and stared at the man on the stage. He was so handsome and kind, and she couldn't deny the love she saw reflected in his eyes as he watched her from the podium. Her world, his world, it didn't matter—they were the same, and their love for each other would be the same anywhere.

LOGAN TRIED TO scan the crowd while he read, but his gaze continued to return to Leigh. How could he look anywhere else when the woman he was in love with was sitting in a far booth, looking more beautiful than he'd remembered? She was here. Losing his place on the page in front of him, he stuttered. "Sorry…can't read my writing…" he said, the private joke earning him a smile from Leigh, further throwing off his focus. Finding his place, he continued on…in a rush. He couldn't wait to be done. She was here.

He cut the excerpt short. If they wanted to know what happened next, they could buy the damn book. "Thank you," he said, closing the book and handing it to Gina, who looked annoyed.

From the bar, Clive shook his head and rolled his eyes.

Whatever. His agent was the only one in the room who knew the scene actually continued.

Stepping off the podium, he made his way through the congratulatory crowd to Leigh. "Hi," he said when he finally reached her.

"That was an odd place to stop," she said with a smile.

"Ah, these people only come for the free

alcohol anyway. So…how are you?" The question was a loaded one as he was desperate to hear about her grandmother and the adoption process.

"I'm good."

"How's your grandmother feeling?"

"She's much better. I think the heart attack scared her, though. She's not working alone in the bakery anymore and she's decided to move into the seniors' complex in town."

"That's probably a good thing." He knew it would help take some of the pressure off Leigh. He smiled at her, the joy of seeing her so strong, he couldn't tear his eyes from her face. Suddenly he felt far too far away from her. "May I?" he asked, gesturing to the other side of the booth where she sat.

"Please," she said, moving over quickly to make room.

He took her hand in his as he sat and studied her. "I'm sorry, I don't mean to keep staring like this. I just can't believe you're here. I mean, when we said goodbye at the B-and-B, I thought that was it."

"Me, too. And I wasn't sure coming here

was the right thing…but I wanted to see you. The truth is—"

His cell phone rang loudly in his coat pocket, startling them both.

Stupid phone. "Please, go on."

"Don't you have to get that?"

"No."

"It might be important."

"This is more important," he said, but as soon as the call went to voice mail, the phone rang again.

"The person on the phone seems to believe differently. It's okay, go ahead."

Logan grumbled as he pulled out his phone. "Someone better be dying," he mumbled; then his heart stopped at the sight of his ex's number.

"Everything okay? You look pale," Leigh said, touching his arm.

"It's Kendra. They were arriving in New York tonight for the court case on Monday morning." They were here. Amelia was in the city. Excitement and nerves overwhelmed him as he continued to stare at the ringing phone.

"Answer it!" Leaning over him, she accepted the call. "Sorry," she whispered.

Logan slowly brought the phone to his ear. "Hello?"

"Hi, Dad," Amelia's excitement made his eyes water.

"Hi, baby girl. How was the flight?"

"Long. Where are you?"

"At my book-launch party. Remember, I told you about it last week?"

"Can I come?"

The bar was eighteen-plus and it was almost nine. "Sorry, sweetie, it's adult only." He couldn't wait to see her, but Leigh was here.

"But Mom said I'd see you tonight." Her disappointment was so tough to hear.

"I know, sweetie."

"Go see her," Leigh whispered, touching his hand.

Logan hesitated. This could be the last time he saw Leigh, who'd come all the way from Brookhollow. But his daughter was finally back in New York…and she wanted to see him.

"Tell her you're on your way," Leigh insisted.

"Dad?" Amelia said on the other end.

"Yes, sweetie, I'm here." He paused, staring at the woman he loved.

"Go," she whispered.

He hadn't known it was possible to love her even more. Squeezing her hand, he mouthed, "Thank you" before saying, "Tell your mom to drop you off in fifteen minutes."

"ARE YOU SURE?" Logan asked her again outside the bar.

"Are you kidding me? Yes! Go see your little girl," Leigh said, desperately striving to hide her disappointment.

"I'm nervous and excited, and disappointed that I have to go right now," he said, touching her cheek.

"Nervous?" She understood the other two. She was feeling them, too.

"Yeah. I mean, it's been over a month since I've seen her."

"She's missed you just as much as you've missed her." She believed that. Though she suspected he did have a tough battle ahead of him with his ex in court Monday morning.

"Thank you." He kissed her hand.

Leigh checked her watch. After nine. "You better go."

After consulting his own watch, Logan nodded, but instead of turning away, he pulled her close. He slid his arms around her waist, and she tilted her face upward until their lips met. This time she accepted the kiss wholeheartedly, not wanting it to end. His arms tightened around her and he drew her even closer. She leaned into him and savored his lips on hers. When he reluctantly pulled away a moment later, he buried his face in her hair, still holding her close. "If only life weren't so complicated."

"It's fine, really," she said, forcing a carefree tone she didn't feel.

"We'll figure this out…we have to," he said, determination in his dark eyes.

She nodded. She knew he meant it.

"I promise," he said.

She nodded again, not trusting her voice.

"You're sure you're okay with this?"

"Of course." She forced a smile. "Go, it's getting late."

"Okay, well…"

"I'll see you when I see you?" she said,

noticing this time she'd allowed herself just enough hope to say "when," not "if."

"Yes." He took a step toward her and placed a tender kiss on her forehead. "And I promise, you will see me…soon."

"DAD, AM I GOING to have to go back to L.A.?" Amelia asked an hour later as he turned off her bedroom light. Having her back in her room after a month of short phone calls was wonderful. She seemed as happy to be here.

Pausing at the door, Logan struggled to find the words to answer his daughter's question. If only he knew. "Do you want to?" he asked, going back into the room and taking a seat next to her bed. He realized it was probably the first time either he or Kendra had asked for the girl's input.

"Not really. I mean, it's warm there and the beach was nice…but the kids at school weren't very friendly."

He brushed her dark curls away from her tiny face. "Changing schools can be tough." He knew that firsthand. He also knew that people were different out West.

Not better or worse, just different, and it would be a big change for his child.

"I'd rather stay here with you," she said quietly, "but then I feel guilty about leaving Mom."

Logan sighed. This was all far too much to put on the shoulders of an eight-year-old and he wished Kendra could think about their daughter's feelings and future for once.

"You shouldn't feel guilty, sweetheart. Your mom wants to be in L.A. and that's her decision," he said, fighting to keep his disdain for Kendra's choices from his voice. Since their separation, they'd tried—or at least he had tried—to never let the girl feel animosity from him toward her mother. "And if a judge decides on Monday that L.A. is where you should be, too, then I'll be there, as well." It annoyed him that one person's decision could affect them all so much and there was nothing he could do about it.

"What about your books and stuff?" she asked. His little girl definitely hadn't inherited her mother's selfishness and she was far too smart.

"What's important is that we're together, and I'll make sure that happens, okay?" Leaning forward, he kissed her cheek. "Now get some sleep. We'll go to the park in the morning and get ice cream from Kerbs." The ice-cream café at the edge of the park was a tradition of theirs and he wanted to make sure the following day in the city was as special as it could be…just in case.

"I'm actually trying to watch my sugar intake. Do they have frozen yogurt?" she asked.

Watching her sugar intake…Logan shook his head. Clearly a month in L.A. with her mother had already been too long. Ruffling her hair, he said, "You're getting ice cream—a double scoop…in a waffle cone…with whip cream and sprinkles." He tickled her and she giggled.

He'd missed that sound so much. "Good night, honey," he said, once more heading for the door.

"I love you, Dad."

"I love you more. Sleep tight."

LOGAN PACED THE hallway in the courthouse, outside the deliberation room late

Monday morning. He hadn't been able to sit in the stuffy room any longer while they waited for a verdict from the judge. He replayed the morning's proceeding, searching for a reason why things wouldn't go his way. The judge had been a fan of his work, which had been a blessing and a major annoyance to Kendra, but Logan doubted the man's book preference would sway his judgment on their futures.

The fact that they'd never been married had been Kendra's lawyer's major case, and while his own lawyer, Eric James, tried to reassure him that these days the courts put less emphasis on those things and focused more on the best interests of the child, Logan was frantic. How many times over the past five weeks had he regretted their decision not to have gotten married?

The door opened, and Eric joined him in the hallway. "How are you holding up?"

"This is killing me. Seriously, how long are they going to keep us waiting?"

"Unfortunately it could take some time. Your case isn't as simple as most. Relocation of one party with the child is a lot to take into consideration," Eric said, checking his watch. "I was going to grab a coffee while there's time. You want anything?"

"No, thanks." His mouth was dry and his stomach turned, but he knew he'd never keep anything down. His nerves were getting the better of him and he felt sick.

The bailiff opened the door and waved them back inside. "Judge is ready," he said.

"So much for coffee," Eric said. "Ready?"

"No." Now that he was about to hear the decision, he almost wished that it had taken longer. His chest was tight and his palms were sweating as they took their place in the front of the courtroom. Across the room, Kendra texted on her phone, avoiding his gaze.

It still amazed him how much things had changed between them. Though he was coming to realize that things hadn't changed; he'd just started to see them for what they were. He finally saw her as she was instead of the person he'd fallen in love with. Unfortunately his daughter was suffering the consequences of their failure more than any of them. He was glad Kendra hadn't brought her to the courthouse that morning. The last thing he'd wanted was for his little girl to see this.

"All rise, court is in session, the Honorable Judge Casey presiding," the bailiff said as the judge entered.

The room spun around him as the judge started to speak and he gripped the edge of the table. His future rested on what this man was about to decide.

"Take a breath, man," Eric whispered.

"In the case of Walters versus Kelland, I have decided that in the best interest of Amelia Kelland, joint legal custody is awarded to both parents," the judge said.

"Joint legal?" Logan asked quietly.

"Equal responsibility for decision making," Eric explained in an aside.

"As for where the child will reside, that depends on you, Ms. Kelland," the judge said. "Do you intend to return to New York City if custody is awarded to Mr. Walters or remain in L.A.?"

She hesitated, glancing toward him. "In L.A., Your Honor," she said.

Unbelievable. Logan held his breath. *Please.*

"In that case, given the fact that Mr. Walters had been the primary caregiver until the dissolution of the relationship, and had shared time with the child after the separation, and based on the child's letter expressing her desire to remain with her father, Amelia Kelland will reside with Mr. Walters with eight weeks visitation a year awarded to Ms. Kelland in L.A..."

Overcome with relief, he didn't hear anything else.

"Congratulations, Logan."

Turning to his lawyer, he shook his hand. "I can't thank you enough."

His daughter was staying with him in New York. He didn't have to move.

At least not to L.A.

"So, SHE CAN CALL?" Kendra asked outside the courtroom half an hour later. Her mascara-stained cheeks were the only real sign that she was upset by the judge's verdict as her tone remained cool, distant.

"I'll get her a cell phone and she can call or text anytime." Not just once a week, he added silently.

"Okay." She removed an invisible piece

of lint from her dark gray jacket and shifted the weight of her purse on her shoulder. "As for the visits…I'm not sure when… I mean if I get the part I auditioned for last week…"

She couldn't be serious. The woman had just found out that she would have eight weeks a year with her daughter and she wasn't sure when she'd have time?

"Please stop looking at me like I'm the most terrible person in the world."

Was he? He shook his head but remained silent. He'd spent many years stroking Kendra's ego. It wasn't his responsibility anymore.

"Logan, I don't expect you to understand. You get to live your dream. What about mine?" It was an argument he'd heard too many times. His success had only served as a thorn in her side as she'd tried to make a name for herself.

"Mine doesn't come at the cost of Amelia's wellbeing. Besides, we both know I'd give up mine in a heartbeat if it meant a better future for her."

Over the years he'd struggled not to judge Kendra's choices, but if she was asking for his permission this time, she wasn't going to get off so easy. He was happy that his daughter was staying with him, instead of being raised by a nanny in L.A. while her mother chased an elusive dream, but his heart ached for his daughter who would undoubtedly miss her mother, despite their differences.

Her voice cracked as she said, "She's so proud of you. She talks about you all the time and she tells all her friends how her dad is a bestselling author. I want her to be proud of me, too."

She was a good actress, he'd give her that. Unfortunately he'd seen this woe-is-me act from his ex before. "Kendra, you're going to do what you're going to do. You've never needed my permission."

"Just give me a year, Logan. Just twelve months in L.A. to see if I can make this happen. If not…" Her voice trailed off as she wiped the tears off her cheeks. "I'm not getting any younger. It's now or never."

"Your daughter's not getting any younger, either, and forgive me for my bluntness, but I think she needs her mother more than Hollywood does."

Squaring her shoulders, she checked her watch. "I assume it's okay that she stay with me at my parents' place for the next few weeks, before I need to head back?"

"Of course." He had a lot of things he needed to take care of, and two weeks would give him enough time to put together a new future for him and his daughter.

As Kendra walked away, all the stress and anxiety of the last month melted away and he released a deep breath.

He thought of Leigh, kind and caring, and he grinned.

There was a day-care sign he needed to hang three hours away, and he couldn't wait to get back there to do it.

"MISS LEIGH, COME QUICK, it's snowing!" Isabel yelled from the living room window two weeks later.

All six kids and Leigh made their way to the nearest windows to peer outside. It wouldn't surprise her if it was in fact snowing. The temperature drop in the past few weeks had been significant and they'd woken up to a frost-covered morning more than once that week already. She pulled back the living-room curtain, but she didn't see snow. "Are you sure?"

"Yes," the little girl said. "I definitely saw snowflakes."

Leigh waited. Nothing. "Do any of you see them?" she asked the other kids, eagerly waiting with their tiny noses pressed to the glass. She couldn't help laughing at how excited they all were for the first sign of snow in Brookhollow. How easily they forgot from year to year how by late January they were lamenting the heavy white powder. Or how stir-crazy they all became cooped up indoors during those freezing temperatures.

"No," they chorused, losing interest and moving away from the window.

Isabel pouted. "I saw one flake at least."

"I believe you," Leigh said, letting the curtain fall. "Come on, it's lunchtime." Wrapping an arm around the girl's shoulder, she led the way to the kitchen, where Ashley served homemade chicken soup and grilled cheese sandwiches. Helping them onto their chairs and handing out napkins, Leigh said, "After we eat, I thought we could gather leaves from the yard before the snow does arrive to make construction-paper turkeys for your families for Thanksgiving." The holiday was just ten days away and she was determined to focus on the good. Be grateful for all the great things in her life and not think about the disappointments over the last month. Her grandmother was feeling much better and her parents would be spending the holiday with them in Brookhollow. Everything else would come…eventually. In the meantime, she had a lot to be thankful for. "Ashley, can you stay with the kids for a few moments? I'm just going to run outside," she said, leaving the kitchen. The girl's snow viewing might have been premature, but the snow was on its way and she still hadn't hung her day-care sign. Of course, it had nothing to do with the fact that it had been almost over two weeks since she'd heard from Logan and she was starting to lose hope.

Outside moments later, she placed the rickety ladder against the side of her house and, tucking the day-care sign under her arm, she hesitated before stepping onto the first rung of the ladder. The wind blew, knocking it against the side of the roof. Maybe this wasn't such a great idea. She bit her lip as she pulled her jacket higher around her neck, shivering in the cold, violent November wind. But if she didn't hang it now, it would be spring before she would have another opportunity. Besides, it had been her fault Logan had fallen from this ladder, not the ladder's.

"Don't tell me you're actually thinking about climbing that old thing again?" Logan's voice behind her made her heart race. As she turned slowly to face him, her mouth fell open and she couldn't find her voice.

Logan wore a small grin on his slightly scruffy face as he came closer. His unshaven face reminded her of the day they'd met, but unlike that day, there was no trace of pain or anger in his expression. No, this time she saw only love so pure it almost stopped her heart.

"Seriously, Leigh. I refuse to break any more bones for you." He brushed her dark hair away from her face. "I just got the first cast removed."

She looked at the hand caressing her face. The cast was gone. "What are you doing here?" she finally choked out.

"Do you realize that in all the time that you and I were falling in love, I never thought to ask for your phone number?"

Her mouth gaped. No! She thought hard. He was right. He'd never needed it. They had always just met at the gazebo every evening at six. And her home number was unlisted. All this time thinking that he wasn't calling because he'd started to forget about her…

"We are seriously two of the most oblivious people in the world," he said, taking her into his arms and gently kissing the top of her head. "And I've been so desperate to hear your voice this last week I couldn't wait to get back here."

She moved closer, enjoying the warmth of his embrace; then remembering, she pulled back. "How did it go in court?" She held her breath, praying for the best possible news.

Logan's wide smile spoke volumes as he nodded. "I was granted joint custody."

She released a sigh of relief as tears of

happiness formed in her eyes. "Logan, that's great." Joint custody…not full? She glanced around him. He was alone. Her smile faded.

"Yes, it is. Joint legal custody, meaning Kendra has equal say in decision making…but despite the verdict, she has decided to still move to L.A. So Amelia's going to live with me full-time…here in Brookhollow."

Leigh's knees buckled under her and he caught her before she fell. "Oh, thank—Wait, you want to move to Brookhollow?"

"Actually, Leigh, I kind of already have," he said, motioning at the pickup truck parked a few houses away. In the bed was a writing desk and lots of boxes.

Leigh laughed. "That's all you have?"

"It's all I needed from New York. Everything else was here…or will be this weekend when Kendra brings Amelia before she leaves for L.A. I even have a place to live already."

"You do?"

"Yes. Apparently the apartment above the bakery was just recently vacated."

"You spoke to Grandma Norris? You're renting her apartment?"

"Hopefully it will be my *office* sooner rather than later, but yes. I called the bakery to get your number from her and she refused to give it to me."

Leigh's eyes widened. "She did?"

Logan nodded. "She said if I had something to say, I'd better get my butt back here and say it. She was right." Taking her hand, he led her toward the truck. "I did pick up one other item on my way into town." Logan turned her around in his arms and cradled her against his chest as he pointed.

Leigh smiled at the new ladder in the bed of the truck, wrapped in a big red bow. "That's for me? How romantic," she said through a laugh.

"I don't buy a new ladder for just anyone."

He was moving to Brookhollow.... The idea was hard to believe. Everything she ever wanted was suddenly so close. "Um... Logan, are you sure about this?"

"Leigh, I have never been so sure about any decision I've made in my life. I thought

Brookhollow was just a place to hide… then you…then this town… This is the first place I feel I truly belong. And I've told Amelia about everything, and she's excited." He turned her to face him, and cupped the back of her neck with his hand. As his mouth descended to hers again, she placed a finger against his lips.

"Wait."

"What's wrong?"

Nothing. For the first time everything was right, even for just a moment. She hoped what she was about to tell him didn't change that. "I still want to pursue the adoption. It might take years or it could be months, but…you need to know that before you make any decisions about your future or Amelia's."

"Shh. *You* are the person who makes this decision the right one, no matter what challenges it brings with it. We'll do this adoption process together—as a family."

She hugged him tightly and in his big, strong arms she felt all her years of disappointment drift away, all the years of sadness and longing. "I love you," she whispered.

"I love you, too. Does this mean I get to actually see the inside of your house now?" he said, taking her hand as they made their way back to her garden.

"I'm not sure," she said, pretending to think. "I mean, what will people say around town?"

"They will say, 'Happiness looks beautiful on Leigh.'"

* * * * *